BARE

———

A HOLLYWOOD ROMANCE

SARAH ROBINSON

Bare © 2018, Sarah Robinson

Editing by Katherine Tate, Author and Editor

Cover Design by Marianne Nowicki at PremadeEbookCoverShop.com

Represented by Literary Agent Nicole Resciniti, The Seymour Agency

*To anyone who has ever lost their dream
and fought like hell to earn it back.*

CHAPTER ONE

"I QUIT." Reed Scott's agent looked at him and tossed the tabloid magazine in his face. "Literally. I fucking quit."

Reed slumped farther down in the plush arm chair in the agency's office. "Jason, I already apologized. What more do you want? It's not like I asked to be followed around L.A. every goddamn second of my life."

His agent's claims of quitting were something he'd heard a dozen times before, but that didn't stop the guilt from getting to him. He liked his agent, in fact, they were pretty good friends. Making his job even harder certainly wasn't what Reed wanted, and yet, he couldn't seem to help himself. The paparazzi were everywhere, even when he was sure that he was alone. They always seemed to find a way to catch him on tape.

"*Bad Boy Reed Scott Caught Licking Tequila Off Stripper's Stomach,*" Jason read the headline on the front of the tabloid out loud. "Oh, or what about this one? *Party Animal Reed Scott Has A Sleepover—In a Sorority!* I mean, are you trying to give me a heart attack? Are you trying to sleep your way through all of L.A.?"

Reed scoffed, rolling his eyes. He hadn't slept with the entire sorority, for Christ's sake. They just picked the most salacious headlines to sell their stupid tabloids. Hell, ninety percent of the things they reported about him, he'd never even done. It was the few photos that they managed to get that fucked him over. "Well, what's the plan? Isn't there something we can do to get them to pull the articles?"

"This isn't a TV show, Reed. I can't just wish away your scandals in sixty minutes or less." Jason finally sat down in the leather chair behind his large mahogany desk. "We need damage control. We need PR. We need an entirely new brand."

"All right." He knew the drill on that one. Half his career had been fucking up and the other half had been fixing the first half. "Kiss some babies? Donate some money to charity?"

Jason shook his head. "Not even close to enough. With this new moving coming up, we're going to need to drastically change your image. *Break Down* is a romantic dance film. That means it's geared toward teens and young girls who want to see a heartthrob —not someone who stuck his dick in all their friends."

Reed grimaced at the comparison. His agent was definitely exaggerating heavily, but there was some truth to the fact that he had spent the majority of his career enjoying the perks of fame. Hitting it big on a small film out of college that blew up into a box-office smash, Reed's acting career had been skyrocketing ever since.

With fame and money came women. It had been hard to resist the attention, and even harder to resist all the gorgeous women who had thrown themselves at him. Sure, he'd turned down plenty, but he'd said yes to plenty more. None of them lasted more than a few dates, though. He'd tried—seriously tried —to put in the time and effort to find a lasting relationship, but every time he found someone he thought might be the girl to help him forget...forget *her*...he went running the other direction.

As much as he wanted to forget the woman he'd fallen in love with over a decade ago, he couldn't...and if he was being honest, maybe he didn't want to forget her at all. So, the other women? They were just Band-Aids, holding him together because losing her had already broken him apart.

And knowing it was all his fault? That was something he'd never forgive himself for.

"The first thing you can do? Put your dick back in your pants. No more women." Jason pulled out a legal pad and began scribbling on it. "I'm going to call some publicists, see what we can do about getting you in front of the lens in a positive way. Probably a few photo shoots, some lunches with clean-cut celebs, a few appearances at charity functions. We need to rebrand your image —who you are."

Who I am? Good luck, because Reed wasn't even sure what the answer to that one was. "Fine. Whatever we need to do."

Despite his propensity for enjoying the finer things in life, Reed was one of the hardest working actors in Hollywood, and he had zero plans on changing that now. If he needed to fix his shit, he was going to fix his shit. This movie was important, and he was going to put everything he had into it. Acting wasn't just a career for him, but an art form. It was something he'd been passionate about his whole life, from being in plays and productions in high school, to starring in indie films in college. He'd spent years honing his craft, and while he might act like a dick off set every once in a while, when those lights came on, he was pure professional.

"But while I'm working on this—you're cleaning up your act. Get to set, practice every fucking minute of the day, and stay away from booze, parties, and women." Jason pointed a finger at him. "Got it?"

"Christ, you sound like my father or something." The irritation in Reed's voice was barely masked. They were friends, but, damn, how many lectures did he really need? Were a few nights partying really that big a deal? At least he wasn't a drug addict or into some of the other heavy shit he'd seen actors lose themselves to. "I understood you the first time. I'm going to the set right after here, so I'm sure I'll be plenty busy."

Understatement of the year. He still couldn't believe he'd been cast on a film completely centered around dance. That wasn't his background or expertise at all, and yet, somehow, he was going to have to dazzle women with sexy choreography.

"Fuck this up, and I swear I'm going to quit," Jason reminded him for the zillionth time. Honestly, Reed wasn't sure why he hadn't just quit by now. "Get the hell out of my office and go make us some money."

Reed laughed at that one, mainly because that was the only reason he'd agreed to sign on to a film where he'd have to learn to dance. The pay was phenomenal, and while he loved acting for its craft, there was no doubt that he loved those seven-figure checks just as much.

A few minutes later, he was climbing into his Lexus and heading for the studio where he'd be spending most of the next three months filming *Break Down*. A young production assistant met him at the gate. She gave him a tour of the lot, and then finally showed him to his trailer near the main set. It was even nicer than his contract had specified, and basically felt like a small luxury apartment.

She giggled when she showed him the bedroom to the back of the trailer, running her hand against the mattress cover. "It's really soft. We made sure of that for you."

"Thanks," he said, not blind to the fact that her eyes were raking over his body like he was someone she wanted to devour. *No women.* He'd promised his agent that literally less than an hour ago. "What time do I report to set?"

The production assistant lifted her clipboard and examined

her notes. "Thirty minutes. Is there anything I can get you in the meantime? I'll be your go-to for anything you need." Her flirty smile returned. "Seriously, anything you need...I can do."

Reed nodded his head. "I appreciate it, but I'll be fine. I think I'm going to walk around set for a bit, get a feel for the place."

"Okay," she replied, looking a bit disappointed. "I'm one call away if you need me." With that, she left him alone in the trailer.

Heading back to the bedroom, he examined the drawers and realized they were already filled with his clothes and personal items. Picking out a black T-shirt that showcased his perfectly defined arms and chest, Reed changed into that and a pair of jeans before walking back out onto the set.

"Reed!"

He turned his head to see the director calling him over. "Hey," he greeted him, shaking his hand when he got closer. "How are you, Mario?"

Mario Cruz, the director for *Break Down*, smiled at a him. "Good. Good to see you here. You all settled into your trailer?"

"Yeah. It's gorgeous."

Mario looked relieved. "Fantastic." A young woman in bright blue leggings was walking past, and Mario flagged her down. "Have you met Taylor? She's our second female lead. Plays Alexandra, and she's a fantastic dancer."

"Nice to meet you," Reed said, offering his hand.

She shook it. "You, too! Have you met Elena yet? She's your lead."

"I have," he replied. "We met during initial contracts."

Taylor smiled, sweet and friendly and nothing at all like the other women he'd run into today who'd acted like they wanted to eat him alive. "Great! Well, I have to run. My wife is waiting for me."

Reed smiled, glad he would be working with such a friendly cast. "See you later."

"Hey, I want you to meet someone else," Mario announced, turning and waving at another woman a few dozen feet away. "Hey, Teagan! Come meet Reed!"

The woman turned to face them, her thick, light brown hair falling over her shoulder as her dark brown eyes found his. Her eyes widened, her full lips parting in surprise...and then, anger? She knit her brow and set her jaw, and Reed realized who he was looking at.

His stomach fell, his shoulders tightening as the lithe young woman walked over to them.

"Reed Scott," she called him by his full name when she got closer. "We've met."

He had no idea what to say to the woman he'd been thinking about every day for over a decade. "Teagan..."

"You two already know each other?" Mario asked, squeezing his shoulder. "Well, good. That'll make it even easier to work together. Teagan is our set choreographer and she'll be working with you every morning before filming starts to learn the moves for that day."

Easier. It would be anything but. Not to mention the fact that Teagan was looking at him like she wanted to murder him. He deserved it, that was for sure, but it didn't make it any easier to see hate in the eyes of the woman he'd once loved.

"I look forward to it, though, I'm not the greatest dancer," he admitted, trying to break the ice. "You'll have your work cut out for you."

She lifted one brow, crossing her arms over her chest. "I think I'll manage."

The way she stood, all her weight resting on one athletically toned leg and her hip jutting out. It was full of personality and every bit the Teagan he remembered. The years hadn't done a thing to her beauty, and the fire in her eyes only seemed to make her more attractive. She was wearing a tight gray leotard over an even tighter pair of black leggings.

She'd always been a dancer, even back when they'd first dated, she'd been headed for fame and fortune with her skills. He'd never followed her career, or even looked her up, since they'd parted ways. He couldn't; it had been too painful to even think of her. But, he was a bit surprised to see her on set as a choreographer. He'd always pictured her on a stage, or starring in a film just like this one. She'd had the talent for it.

"Well, I'm ready to get started when you are," he offered.

"Great! Glad you two are hitting it off." Mario gave them both a pat on the back and then walked away.

Teagan nodded her head slowly, as if evaluating Reed's sincerity. "Tomorrow morning. Six o'clock. Studio B off the back lot."

"I'll be there." Reed paused for a moment, running his tongue across his bottom lip. "Hey, Teagan?"

"Hmm?" She let her arms drop to her sides, and for a moment, she looked vulnerable, like the Teagan he'd once known—the one who didn't hate him.

"I'm happy to see you again." He let his gaze dip to her lips, the way she nibbled on the edge when she was nervous. He remembered everything about her, about the way she moved, the way she loved. "Really happy."

"Well, at least one of us is." And with that, she walked away.

CHAPTER TWO

AM I CURSED? Teagan stared at herself in the mirror of her small apartment bathroom. She felt cursed. Reed-Scott-freaking-cursed.

Life certainly hadn't handed her the easiest go, and now, just when she'd thought things were finally turning around because she'd landed a fantastic job as a film choreographer, fate was still proving it had other plans for her. This job was supposed to be her big break—well, break-*ish*. Sure, it wasn't what she'd wanted out of her life, but her dreams were no longer an option.

And this job? Most people would kill for it. So, she was choosing to be grateful.

She had to choose to be grateful a lot, actually. If she didn't, then life would have gotten the better of her years ago. Teagan glanced down at her legs, tracing a finger across the long scar that stretched from her knee to her hip. She tried to hide it under leggings and skirts, but it wasn't always possible.

When she'd almost died in a car accident at the age of twenty-one, she'd thought she'd never walk again. Hell, the doctors had told her exactly that. And dancing? That was an impossibility.

The years and years she'd spent training to become a professional dancer had all been wiped away in less time than it took for that car to slam hers into a ditch. Despite the doctor's predictions that her wheelchair would become a permanent fixture, though, she'd proved them all wrong. She'd spent years learning to walk, and then dance, again. Sure, she'd probably never have the agility to become the famous dancer she'd always dreamed of being, but she could at least teach. And with that, she'd found a way to keep doing what she loved...even if it was not *exactly* what she loved.

So, she chose to be grateful.

But seeing Reed Scott again? The man who made her believe in everlasting, soul-deep, earth shattering love and then left her standing alone at the altar on their wedding day? The man who had left her just to star in a movie that would make him famous?

She was not grateful for that—or for *him*—one bit.

Teagan finished putting on the last touches of her makeup then changed into a new pair of leggings and a leotard. Glancing one last time in the mirror, she fluffed out her wavy brown hair nervously. As much as she might hate him, she found herself wanting to look her best for him anyway. Make him eat his heart out. Make him regret ever leaving her like that in the first place.

She swallowed, trying to push away her frustration. That didn't seem possible right now, though. Sighing, Teagan grabbed her car keys off the small table by her front door and gave one last glance around the small Los Angeles apartment she called home. Benson, her incredibly fat tabby cat, was lounging on the windowsill, lazily yawning and watching her. "Bye, Benson. Be good."

He didn't even blink at her. He'd probably still be lying in that exact same spot when she came home later.

Teagan blew him a kiss then headed out, locking her front

door carefully behind her. Within a few minutes, she was behind the wheel of her car and heading toward the studio. It was still dark outside, but she didn't mind one bit. She enjoyed early mornings when the world was quiet and the roads were clearer. Driving was still something that made her a little tense after her car accident, and traffic in Los Angeles was always horrendous. But, at five o'clock in the morning, it was a lot more manageable and didn't make her feel so...terrified.

Luckily, her commute was short and she arrived on set twenty minutes later. She headed straight to the studio where she'd told Reed to meet her, but he wasn't there yet, which she'd expected since she was a bit early. Placing her dance bag on the shelf to one side of the studio, she pulled out her heel dancer shoes with a cute buckle T-strap over the top of her foot and put them on. She pulled on a loose fitting, light sweater over her leotard for some coverage, since it reached almost to the bottom of her ass.

Next, she began to shimmy out of her leggings, since she was able to work a lot better in her leotard without restriction to her legs. She got down to her knees before she realized that being bare legged would reveal the scar on her leg. Quickly, she slid them back up her legs.

"Shit."

Teagan whirled around, looking for the person who'd just broken the silence around her.

Reed Scott. Of course.

"You scared the crap out of me," she told him, grateful that he hadn't been able to see her scar from where he was standing for the brief moment her leggings had been down.

"Sorry," he replied, clearly making an effort to look anywhere but at her. "I didn't know you'd be...uh, I mean, I wasn't expecting..."

She rolled her eyes. Actors were so dramatic. "I'm not getting naked, Reed. I was just, uh, putting *on* my leggings to dance."

"Sure. Right. Yeah." He was rambling, clutching the gym bag over his shoulder. "So, time to get started?"

"Yep. Put your stuff on the shelf and we'll get started," she instructed, doing her best to ignore the butterflies fluttering in her stomach at the very sight of him. Fuck, he looked even better than he'd looked the last time she'd seen him. Tall, broad shoulders, olive skin under thick black hair with a scruffy beard she remembered was very soft. And those eyes...God, the way those light green eyes pierced through her.

He stood you up at the altar, she reminded herself. *For a damn movie.*

"Sure." He headed toward her and placed his bag on the shelf. "What are we practicing today?"

"It's a pretty short routine today, actually. It shouldn't take us too long." Though she doubted he'd be the quickest learner after his warning yesterday. "Ready?"

He turned around to look at her, his eyes trailing down her body in a way that made her heart pound faster and faster. Suddenly his gaze stopped, pausing on her legs.

Her heart pounded, terrified he could see through her thin leggings to the bump of her scar. But he said nothing, and his gaze kept traveling. She was safe.

Honestly, she was a little surprised he didn't already know about her accident. It hadn't been a secret. Everyone in her life knew, and she'd certainly expected *someone* to pass along the message. Or for him to check in, even once.

She'd waited for him in the hospital, expecting him to come. Expecting him to apologize. Expecting him to beg her forgiveness, realize what an idiot he had been and take her back, care for her, return her to health with his love and affection.

That hadn't really worked out.

Finally, his eyes returned to his face, and his tongue slid across his bottom lip. "You look...damn, Teag. You look amazing."

"Listen, Reed," she began, setting her jaw and sticking out her chin. "We work together. That's it. You don't get to look at me like that anymore."

Reed looked startled, taken aback at her abruptness. Then the saddest look she'd ever seen passed over his face. "You're right. I'm sorry."

"Let's get started." She moved to the center of the studio. "I'll show you today's sequence, and then we'll go through it step by step. Okay?"

He nodded, but said nothing.

Carefully, she posed herself in the center of the room with her toes pointed and her arms around her waist. In one slick move, she sidestepped and kicked one leg out to her left, flipping her hair with the motion. She then tucked her foot, her knee pointed out horizontally from her body and spun in a circle.

On her second spin around, she kicked up high, like an incredibly tall karate kick. When her foot touched back down on the ground, she lunged to the right and threw her arms out, tossing back her head with the motion. She curved her spine outwards, pulling her stomach in as she moved her arms in a circular motion toward herself.

She twirled then, spinning on the tips of her toes while keeping her eyes on one stationary spot so she didn't get dizzy. After her fourth spin, she shoved her arms down by her sides and lifted her chin. With that, she spun back in the direction she'd just come from and leaped multiple times across the room with her arms out and her fingers pointed.

Finally, she came down on one foot and spun in several circles before coming to a stop in front of Reed. "Annnnnd, that's it."

"Shit, that looked complicated as hell," he admitted. "Though you looked incredible doing it."

She ignored his compliment. Or, rather, she tried. Admittedly, her heart pounded a little harder. But, that was being ignored for now. "Let's go over the first step." She repeated the side steps and kicking her leg to the left. "Just like that. Let's see what you can do."

Reed followed in her footsteps, and honestly, it wasn't terrible. It wasn't great either. "Like that?"

"Close," she admitted. "Let's go through it again."

They went through the first few steps multiple times, and over the course of a few hours, he had the majority of the routine down and almost perfect. She figured even if it wasn't perfect, he was hot enough to capture the audience.

"I think we're pretty good to go," she admitted after five hours of practice. "Filming starts soon anyway."

Reed nodded, panting. "I need a shower. That was a hell of a workout."

Teagan tried not to think about him under the water, lathering soap over his naked body. "Do you feel like you've got the routine down? Feel confident?"

He nodded, though he was still panting. Sweat pooled on his chest and back. He grabbed at the top of his shirt and lifted it over his head. Teagan turned away quickly, not wanting to stare at his eight-pack or that sexy V that dipped into his sweatpants.

"I feel pretty good about it. Will you be at filming?"

She nodded. "Yes, but only for help if needed. You should be able to do this on your own."

"I've got this," he repeated. "You're a good teacher. As talented as I remember. Honestly, I'm..."

"You're what?" She dared him to continue along that line of thinking, after she'd already warned him that he didn't get to know her life anymore.

"Surprised," he finished, his tongue sliding across his bottom lip. "Surprised you're a teacher, or, uh, choreographer. I expected to see you in my position, starring in films. Or on stage. You were headed for Broadway. That role you landed...it was your break-out role."

Don't remind me. She'd turned down the role of a lifetime on Broadway to marry the love of her life. Sure, she hadn't told him that, but she also hadn't expected him not to show up at their wedding.

"Reed," she warned. "Don't. Okay? Just...just don't."

He nodded slowly, but clearly was having a hard time with holding back what he wanted to say. "You're a great teacher, Teag. The best. You just...you never wanted this."

"Well, I do now." She lifted her chin defiantly. "Is that okay with *you?*"

He looked startled at her animosity, but she wasn't sorry. "Yeah. I'm sorry. I'm overstepping." He moved closer to her, like he was walking toward his gym bag, but she knew he wasn't. "I just...I think we should talk. We *need* to talk about everything that happened."

Teagan shook her head. "That moment passed eight years ago, Reed. There's nothing left to talk about. It's over. *We're* over."

"I know," he replied, looking unsure despite his guarantee. "But, like you said, we have to work together."

"And we just did. Pretty well, I might add." She walked over to her bag and grabbed it. "Stop looking for problems where there aren't any, okay? I got over you a long time ago. We're not young kids anymore. Despite my feelings—or whatever they are—for you, we can work together and be professional."

He lifted one brow. "Feelings?"

"Hatred, specifically," she clarified, almost wanting to laugh at the dramatics with which she said it. "And a few dashes of extreme anger."

"Ah, those feelings." He chuckled halfheartedly and rubbed the back of his neck. "Got it. Loud and clear."

"Tomorrow, six in the morning." She slung her bag over her shoulder. "Here. Don't be late."

"I'll be here." He grabbed a fresh shirt from his bag and pulled it on. "See you on set later."

With that, she walked out of the studio and quickly rushed to the closest dressing room, collapsing on the small futon inside. She wasn't even sure whose dressing room this was, but, damn, her heart was still racing. Staring up at the ceiling, she felt the tears slipping down her temples.

She hated that he could still have this effect on her. That she still cared. It'd been eight years, and yet seeing him made it feel like yesterday. Her body still reacted to his exactly like it once had when they'd been together, tangled up in each other regularly. But it was more than the way he looked or the chemistry between them. It was that ease and comfort, which, despite her anger, was undeniably still between them.

Like they still fit as easily now as they once had so many years ago.

Teagan wiped at her eyes, pushing away her tears. She'd cried enough over Reed Scott. He didn't deserve another second of it, and she wasn't going to give it to him. Climbing back up off the futon, she stood and re-centered herself with a deep breath.

She could do this. She could be a professional. She would *not* fall back in love with Reed Scott.

CHAPTER THREE

THE FIRST WEEK of filming was a whirlwind in front of the camera. By six in the morning, Reed was at the studio practicing with Teagan for several hours, then on set filming until close to midnight, then going home and studying his lines for the next day before catching barely three or four hours of sleep—only to repeat the entire cycle again the next day.

"We're going a little tougher today," Teagan informed him when he arrived back on set the following Monday morning. They'd had a break over the weekend, which had given him a small chance to recharge his batteries. "Last week was basic steps, and it's time to ramp it up a notch."

"*That* was basic?" Reed groaned and ran his hand over his forehead. Last week had been damn near impossible, and while he'd gotten a good handle on the moves and been able to perform well on camera, it certainly felt nothing close to basic.

Teagan nodded. "You did well, so I'm sure this won't be as hard as you're thinking."

"Wow, a compliment." Reed smiled, enjoying the short-lived feeling of a nice moment between them. Working together had not been easy—and even that was an under-statement.

Teagan was clearly still angry, which he understood, even if he didn't like it. Standing her up at the altar was the worst day of his life, and to this day, there's nothing he felt more ashamed of than that. He'd had his reasons, but as every day went by, they seemed harder and harder to make sense of. His excuses felt flimsy when he reflected back on everything that had happened.

At the time, he'd thought he was doing the best thing for both of them. They were young, *so* young, and had their entire lives and careers in front of them. Teagan had just been offered an insanely amazing break out role in a Broadway show, and was preparing to turn it all down to marry him. He'd wanted more for her than that—she deserved more than just being his wife and living in the suburbs behind a white picket fence. But they were in love, and there was never a possibility that she'd choose anything over him.

So, he'd made the choice for her.

Then a few days after their wedding day, he was offered a role in a small indie film that he'd thought would go nowhere. The timing seemed like fate—something he had to pursue on the heels of leaving a relationship he'd thought would be his forever.

Surprisingly, the movie won contests and festivals and blew up into one hell of a box office hit. His fame had skyrocketed and he was catapulted into a career he'd longed for but wasn't nearly mature enough for. Hence the partying and women and drinking.

And why he'd never looked Teagan up again.

Still, it bothered him to know she'd lived a whole life in the last eight years without him. She seemed...wounded. He wasn't sure how, but there was a pain underneath her anger toward him that felt like it went deeper. Like it wasn't just him who'd hurt her. There was more he didn't know, but all he really wanted to do was sweep back into her life and fix everything he'd broken.

It was insane he felt that way, especially after so many years apart, but every day he spent around her, he couldn't deny it. Despite the wounds she was hiding, she was every bit the beautiful woman he'd fallen in love with—fiercely hardworking, graceful and poised, and though it had yet to be directed toward him, he'd seen her sweet side with other people. He'd seen her laugh at others' jokes, that perfect melodic laughter he'd thought of so many times over the last eight years.

She was lithe and lively, and despite having been handed a difficult lot in life, she was thriving. Nothing had stopped her, and she hadn't slowed down for even a second. Teagan was a fighter, and right now, she was fighting him.

"I'm a professional, Reed," Teagan reminded him, slipping on a pair of fuzzy leg warmers over her shins and the tops of her shoes. That, plus the leotard, leggings, and loose-fitting shirt she was wearing were incredibly sexy, showing off her curves in all the right ways, but he kept those thoughts to himself. "It's not a compliment. It's just an observation as your choreographer."

"Right, don't let it go to my head, you still hate me, yada yada." Reed rolled his eyes. His irritation with the whole situation was harder to keep under wraps when he was this tired. "I got it, okay? You've made it abundantly clear that you'd rather be anywhere else but here with me."

Teagan looked taken aback for a moment, blinking slowly as she stared at him. "I didn't...I mean, I don't—"

"It's fine," he cut her off, not wanting her to have to apologize. She deserved her anger, but that didn't make it any less difficult for him to deal with daily. "Let's just get started."

She nodded, then walked to the center of the room. "Today, it's a two-person sequence. You'll be dancing these on camera with Elena. I'll show you the choreography, but then you and she will practice more together before this afternoon."

Elena Stravinsky was his female co-star on *Break Down*, and their love story was what carried the plot. She was absolutely gorgeous—blonde, tall, and already well known for her dancing. Being paired with her on set was intimidating because she was thousands of times better at it than he was.

"Got it," he replied, joining her in the center of the room.

Teagan took his right hand in hers, facing him. "Stand still for a moment, but then when I come in and toss my hair, spin me." She took his hand but stood beside him, their arms outstretched as they faced the same direction. With a small leap and graceful spin of her legs through the air, she turned into his body and landed squarely chest to chest. His heart was pounding beneath his ribs, aroused at both the beauty of her movements as well as the closeness with which they stood.

Next, Teagan ran her hands up the sides of his body, the backs of her fingers grazing his uncovered skin until she reached his neck. Anchoring her hands behind his neck, she tipped her head backward and flipped her hair from one side to the other in a dramatic twist of her neck.

Watching her neck elongated, open and supple...he wanted to lean forward and nip at her skin. He wanted to run his tongue from her clavicle up to her ear, and then whisper everything he was really thinking to her.

"Now," she instructed, leaving one hand free for him to grab.

He grasped her fingers in his and lifted her arm over her head, spinning her in a circle and catching her as she dipped backward toward the floor, hooking her leg around his knee and sliding into his body. She was right against him, pressing into him and it was taking everything in him to focus solely on the routine.

"Lift," she said next.

He slid his free hand to her waist and pulled her up and over his head where she delicately moved her arms as if riding a wave. Her knees bent toward him, her legs pressed against his chest. His face was mere centimeters from her stomach, and he found himself struggling more and more with resisting touching every inch of her. He wanted to run his hands across her body in the same way she'd just done to him—even if that had just been choreography.

"Spin, and down."

He turned, spinning them around together, then slowly descending as he slid her body down against his. Her breasts passed by his face, then she was looking at him, and they were pressed so tightly together, he never wanted to let go.

"This is where you'll kiss her..." Teagan's voice was breathless, her eyes flitting from his down to his lips. They paused for a moment, as if unsure whether they should follow the routine exactly...or unsure if they could resist.

Reed lowered his head, giving her the chance to touch her lips to his if she just allowed herself. He wanted her to more than anything. God, he wanted to taste her again, devour every inch of her.

"And then back into a spin," she finished, pushing away and allowing him to raise her arm once more and twirl her away from him. She let go of his hands and took a deep breath. "And that's basically the entire thing."

"Can we go through it again?" he asked, mostly for his own selfish purposes or the fact that he was harder than a rock at having just had his hands all over her, but also because it was going to take some serious acting on his part to make this look as hot with Elena as it felt at that moment with Teagan.

She took a deep breath. "The key to today's scene will be your chemistry with Elena. This dance should have erotic undertones, since it's the first scene where your character is beginning to have feelings for Elena's."

He nodded, aware of the scene he was filming today. It was pretty tame, but the script certainly had its risqué moments. There was a sex scene scheduled for next week that he wasn't looking forward to at all. As sexy as those scenes seemed on film, acting in them was clunky and uncomfortable with dozens of people watching and recording the whole thing.

"I'm ready," he assured her, returning to the original stance they'd started in. "When Elena gets here, we'll make sure it's perfect. It'll be the hottest dance scene the silver screen has ever seen."

Teagan visibly swallowed, something painful flashing through her eyes.

Was that jealousy? Reed was sure it wasn't, but he found himself wishing it was anyway.

"Let's start from the top." Teagan lifted her chin and stretched out her arm toward him. "But this time, give me more."

Reed smiled. She didn't have to ask him twice.

CHAPTER FOUR

"FIVE, SIX, SEVEN, EIGHT..." Teagan mouthed along with Reed and Elena's steps from where she was standing off to the side of the set watching them filming.

Elena slid her hands across Reed's chest, pulling his shirt open as the buttons flew everywhere. She tossed her hair and spun to the side, but he pulled her back, twirling her into his body and dipping her down in the same way he'd done with Teagan just hours ago.

She'd be lying if she said she was enjoying watching their performance. They were great, and their chemistry was undeniable. The movie was going to be a hit based on them alone, but that wasn't where Teagan's mind was.

It was the way Elena rolled her body against his, feeling every inch of him. Memories of dancing in the sheets with Reed years and years ago flooded Teagan's thoughts, and she couldn't push them away. When everything had been perfect...when the future was still stretched out in front of them, and fame and love were so close she just had to reach out and grab them.

The way he felt pressed against her, his lips on hers,

devouring every ounce of her soul as their bodies slid against one another, naked and wanting. He'd done things to her she'd never been able to replicate with a man since. Not that she'd dated a ton since Reed, but she hadn't been celibate either.

There was a reason she was still single though. No one made her stomach flip like when he used to kiss her neck, trailing his tongue along the length of her body. Or the way she'd tremble when his hand slid between her legs and made every part of her come alive. And sometimes...she just missed the way he held her. The way they'd cuddle on the couch after a long day of classes, and how just his very touch could make her feel at home, like she belonged.

There was a comfort to being in love, to knowing that the man on her arms was hers, and she was his. She'd felt that safety with Reed.

She'd trusted him with everything she'd had...and then he'd left.

Now here he was with a leggy blonde all over him, looking hotter than sin, and all she could think about was how he'd felt pressed against her earlier today. *Confusing as fuck.*

"Cut!" Mario jumped up from his chair and walked on to the set. "Great job, Elena. Stellar performance, Reed. What did you think, Teagan? They follow your routine correctly? It looked sexy as hell."

Teagan pushed her shoulders back and nodded. "They were perfect."

Elena grinned, tossing her platinum hair over her shoulder and turning to Reed. She batted her long eyelashes and looked up at him from beneath them. "It's all about having the perfect partner." She trailed a finger down Reed's arm.

Teagan glanced up at him, wondering if he was falling for the starlet's blatant flirting. Reed was staring straight at her, his eyes molten in the way that pierced through her. He didn't even seem to notice Elena.

Teagan swallowed and quickly looked away. It was too much, too intense, and she wasn't ready. She still hated him. *Right?*

"Or the perfect teacher," Reed said, moving away from Elena and closer to Teagan.

Teagan quickly stepped back and cleared her throat. "Right, well, thanks. I'm going to go." She gave them a quick wave and then moved toward the stage door.

"I'll walk you out." Reed was suddenly beside her, his stride matching hers. "It's pretty late at night."

She glanced over at him. "The set is guarded. I'll be fine."

"Indulge me."

She recognized the way he spoke—he wasn't going to back down. "Fine, but I'm just going to grab my bag from the dressing room and go back to my car. That's it. Nothing exciting."

Reed didn't respond, but kept his pace beside her. A few minutes later, they entered her small office that was basically a closet. Nothing fancy, but just a place to store her things while she was on set. A futon, a lamp, a mirror. It was pretty bare bones.

"This is your dressing room?" Reed looked around the tiny room.

She nodded. "What's wrong with it? Holds my stuff just fine."

Again, he didn't respond, but he looked upset. Though, she wasn't sure why it mattered to him.

Teagan packed her bag and pulled on a light coat then grabbed her car keys. "I'm parked in the back lot."

"I'll walk you there," Reed said.

She stared at him for a moment, narrowing her eyes. "Why?"

Reed seemed confused, his brows furrowing. "What do you mean?"

"Why are you walking me to my car?"

He shrugged his shoulders. "It's the right thing to do when you care about someone. Keep you safe."

"Reed..."

"Teagan, don't look for reasons to push me away." Reed walked farther into the dressing room and closed the door behind him, shutting them inside. "Don't pretend we don't both know eight years ago was a mistake—a mistake we could fix now."

Tears pricked at the corners of her eyes as she stood there, not knowing what to say. She was not prepared to have this conversation—not now, maybe not ever. "Reed, don't do this."

"I have to. I honestly can't look at you, or dance with you, for one more day and pretend I can handle this. Seeing you, touching you...it's killing me. I made a mistake, Teag. I made the biggest mistake of my life." Reed took her hands in his, pulling her closer to him. "I'm not asking for everything. I'm not even pushing my luck to ask for a second chance. I'm just asking for forgiveness."

She exhaled in one loud breath, trying to push away the tears that were already sliding down her cheeks. She turned her gaze away from him, trying to will away everything she was feeling. "Reed...you left me on our wedding day. For a movie. We were supposed to chase our dreams together, and you ran after yours alone. You left me behind."

He shook his head emphatically. "A movie? No, Teag...I didn't get that movie offer until days later."

"What?" That made absolutely no sense. He left her to take the movie. He left her to chase fame and money and women. She'd told herself that for years. "You...but...why? If not for the movie, then why? Why did you leave?"

Reed closed the gap between them, pulling her against his chest. "Looking back on it, I don't know what I was thinking. I thought I was doing you a favor...I thought I was helping you not have to choose between Broadway and me. I thought you'd turn down that role to be my wife, and I never wanted to be the man who stood between you and your dreams."

Teagan's eyes widened as she stared at him. Suddenly, she tipped her head back and laughed out loud. Like, deep belly laughter erupting throughout her entire body and bubbling up through her throat. He hadn't wanted to stand between her and her future...and yet, that was exactly what he'd done.

"Okay, now I'm confused," Reed admitted. "What's so funny?"

She shook her head, trying to compose herself. He'd ended things between them so she'd take the Broadway role...that she'd already turned down a week before. She'd been waiting to tell him, to surprise him with the news. If she'd told him a week earlier, she'd be married right now. Her entire life would be different. "Life. Life is damn hilarious."

"Does that mean we're..."

She shook her head. "We're nothing, Reed. If you want forgiveness, you can have that. I forgive you. I forgive you for breaking my heart, but we...we are nothing." Teagan pointed between them, and as harsh as her words were, she was surprised to find that she actually meant them. Now that she knew the truth, a lot of her anger was subsiding, and for the first time, she realized she did forgive him. She wasn't going to spend another day harboring the pain he'd left behind. And yet, that was where it ended between them. She still didn't trust him. She still didn't want to repeat her past mistakes. "We're coworkers, Reed. That's it."

Reed squeezed her hand harder then placed her palm against his chest over his heart. His heart thudded heavily under her touch, and the heat between them mesmerized her. "Teag, don't push me away. I know I'm not the only one who feels the electricity between us."

Teagan swallowed hard. She wasn't going to lie. "Chemistry is never something we lacked, Reed. But chemistry isn't enough for forever."

He lowered his voice, leaning closer to her. "What about right now?" His voice was husky and low, his lips inches from hers. All she would need to do is lift her chin and press her mouth to his and they'd be kissing. God, she remembered his kisses...

A shiver rolled over her, but she couldn't find her words.

"Teagan," he repeated, moving even closer. His lips nearly caressed hers, and for a moment, she wanted to let him. She wanted to kiss him. "If we can't have tomorrow...if we can't have forever...can we have tonight? Can we live in the past for a few hours...and pretend? I don't know how to stay away from you, Teag."

His lips brushed across hers and she leaned into him, unable to refrain from wanting just a little bit more. But he waited. He was waiting for her to say yes, to tonight, to tomorrow...to them. This was the moment she'd been waiting for, for him to come crawling back and beg her forgiveness. She'd dreamed of it, luxuriated in knowing that one day he'd regret what he'd done. One day, he'd want her again and she'd have the last laugh.

And now here she was getting everything she'd dreamed of, and all she felt was more devastated than ever before.

"No," she replied softly, her hand pressing gently against his chest to create more distance between them. "I forgive you, but that's all I can do."

CHAPTER FIVE

———

REED GROANED, rolling over in bed and grabbing at his cellphone that was somewhere on his nightstand.

"Hello?" he answered, putting an end to its incessant ringing.

"You up yet?" Jason's blunt tone came through the phone receiver loud and clear. "I've been calling you for a good fifteen minutes now."

Reed ran a hand over his face, rubbing his forehead and stretching. "I'm getting up now."

"You better fucking hurry," Jason instructed. "I've set up a charity event on set today. You need to be there within the hour. Paps will be there toward the end—look surprised to see them."

"You called photographers?" Reed groaned and sat up, placing his feet on the cold wooden floor of his penthouse apartment in downtown Los Angeles.

"Of course not," he replied. "I just might have mentioned it to someone who would call them. Listen, they're going to be there, so take a shower and put on your good-boy suit and smile those pearly whites for the fucking camera, okay?"

"Got it." Reed hung up the phone, not bothering to say goodbye.

Standing, he headed for the bathroom and pulled off the boxers he was sleeping in. He turned on the shower and waited a minute until the water warmed, then stepped inside. The stream of hot water hit his face and he just stood there, letting it wash over his body.

He'd barely slept the night before, unable to stop thinking about his encounter with Teagan. Honestly, he wasn't sure what had come over him. He'd managed to spend two weeks in her presence without forcing his luck, but last night, he hadn't been able to hold back. The way she'd stood there, watching him and Elena, the undeniable jealousy on her face as she mouthed along to their choreography.

For the first time since she'd reentered his life, he'd seen hope. He'd seen a glimmer of a chance that maybe she'd forgive him, maybe she even still loved him. Then when they were in her dressing room, and he'd seen her tears, her desire, her sorrow— and he knew he was right. She did still love him, somewhere, somehow. But she didn't trust him.

And without trust, there was no hope.

So, he'd spent the night tossing and turning, trying to ignore the throbbing in his chest. Trying to ignore the heartbreak that he'd spent years pushing back and pretending didn't exist. The more he thought about it, staring up at the ceiling all night long, the more he realized that he'd never moved on from Teagan. He'd never grieved their break up because he wouldn't allow himself to.

He still loved her, and he didn't want to stop loving her.

The problem now was that he loved her enough to realize she didn't want him, and he had to respect that. And that fucking sucked. She'd made herself clear, and he wasn't going to push, but damn, he wanted to. He wanted to prove to her how wrong she was, how he'd changed, how he could be everything he'd once promised to her.

Reed lathered shampoo into his hair then rinsed it out under the water. He reached down and grabbed his dick, thinking of how beautiful Teagan had looked dancing against him at their last training. He stroked himself slowly, then began to speed up. He wanted to satisfy the need he'd felt building inside him since the moment she'd first turned around on set and looked at him.

His own climax began to build, and then just as quickly as he started, he stopped. Mid-stroke, he let go and turned the faucet to make the water raining down on him as cold as possible.

Who was he kidding? He wanted to believe he'd changed, or could change for her, but could he? If he believed the latest tabloid covers, it certainly didn't seem like he had. Teagan didn't deserve a man who made covers with a sorority girl's tits bouncing off him. Hell, he didn't even deserve to stand here and jerk off at the very thought of her.

Nothing about him had changed. He was the same guy who'd broken her heart eight years ago. He hadn't deserved her then, and he didn't deserve her now.

Finished with his showering, Reed stepped out from under the water and grabbed a nearby towel. After a quick dry off, he crossed his expansive bedroom and opened the double doors to his closet. Rows and rows of suits and designer clothes greeted him, along with an island in the middle with shoes and watches and other accessories he'd been sent over the years.

He grabbed his phone and dialed the director's number as he walked back into the bedroom. "Mario."

"Hey, Reed. What's going on?" Mario answered when he picked up the line.

"I need a favor."

Mario chuckled. "Well, sure. You're the star. What do you need?"

"The choreographer—her dressing room is barely bigger than a broom closet. She needs a real office and a changing room."

"Uh..." Mario began, stumbling a bit. "Well, we don't usually give crew a ton of space. That's really reserved for the talent."

"She's the best fucking talent you've got on that set." Unable to stop it, Reed found his voice suddenly rising an octave.

"Okay. Okay, I'll...get her a bigger space." Mario sighed. "Tell me nothing is going on between you two, though...right? Jason Allen promised me we'd have no issues with women on set."

Reed rolled his eyes. Of course his agent had cock-blocked him. "She's an old friend. That's it."

"Oh." Mario seemed pleased with that answer. "All right, I'll set it up."

"Thanks, Mario. I appreciate it." With that, Reed hung up.

He headed back into his closet and picked out a "good boy" outfit he was sure his agent would approve of. Despite the fact that it was a weekend, Reed found himself wondering if Teagan would be there. Hell, he'd enjoyed sleeping in today because practicing and filming all week was fucking exhausting, but he definitely missed seeing her.

Forty-five minutes later, Reed was walking on to set and Jason was there waiting for him.

"About time." Jason slapped him on the shoulder. "Come on. You're going to love this."

"What's the charity?" he asked, following him onto the main set.

"Disabled Children Coalition. There's about twenty kids on set, all with different physical disabilities, who want to meet you and take pictures with their favorite actor. Plus, you're going to take them on a tour around set and explain acting and filming and all that." Jason opened the door to the set for him and ushered him inside. "These kids love you, and they've been through a lot. Show them a good time."

"You sound like you think I won't." Reed turned to his agent. "Kinda insulting, man."

"No," Jason assured him. "I've seen you with your niece. You're great with kids."

Reed nodded, because that was definitely the truth. He loved kids, and even more than that, he loved his niece, Nell. He and his younger sister were very close, and had been all their lives. She was often alone since her husband was in the military and currently deployed, so he stepped in as much as he could to help her with Nell.

"You don't need to worry, Jason. I'm turning over a new leaf. No casual sex, no partying. Only work and more work." And that was the truth. He needed to be more serious about his life, and reflecting on his past, on Teagan, had really shown him that. He was going to make changes in his life, starting with cutting out the bad boy reputation he'd earned. "You won't see me on any tabloids anytime soon."

Jason nodded, still looking dubious. "I've got all the faith in you, Reed. You've got this."

Reed could still hear the skepticism in his voice, but he was going to prove it to him. He was going to prove it to Teagan, but most importantly, he was going to prove it to himself.

It was time to expect more from himself.

CHAPTER SIX

—————

Teagan stretched her arms over her head in the empty studio and lifted onto the tips of her toes. She slowly extended one leg to her side, perpendicular from her body and then leaned her torso toward it. Returning to flat feet, she leaped to the side and swirled around, this time with one leg straight up in the air. She turned again and again, circling on one foot with her other leg pressed against her shoulder pointing up at the ceiling.

She monitored her movements in the mirrored wall in front of her, paying close attention to every position of her body and movement of her muscles. Carefully, she made changes to the routine as she watched herself, perfecting every motion until she was satisfied with exactly how she wanted it to look. She'd be training Elena on this routine on Monday, and wanted it ready and concise by then.

Working weekends were a habit for Teagan now. It was easier to prepare choreography for the coming week alone, as well as get her own exercise in. Being that her own apartment was tiny, she had nowhere else but the studio to work.

Finally, she lowered her leg and bent to touch the floor,

stretching out her back. Turning to each side, she elongated her neck and lengthened her spine. Once she felt fully loose, she sat cross-legged on the wooden dance floor and stared at herself in the mirror.

There was something magical about dancing, even alone in an empty room. After her accident, she'd spent almost a year chained to a hospital bed. She hadn't even been able to walk, let alone take care of herself. But she'd been determined.

With extensive physical and occupational therapy, she'd managed to stand, and then take a few steps, and finally...walk. That still wasn't enough for her, though. Teagan smiled at her memory. Her therapists had told her not to get her hopes up. She would never dance again.

And yet, here she was...dancing. She'd always been meant to dance.

Pushing back up to her feet, Teagan wrapped her own arms around herself, feeling a sense of pride in her accomplishments. She grabbed her dance bag and swung it over her shoulder, then exited the studio and headed for the main set since she'd parked over there this morning.

Turning the corner, Teagan saw a group of children walking through the doors to the main set. Some were in wheelchairs, others on crutches. Some had deformities, others were missing limbs entirely. She was startled for a second at the irony of what she'd just been thinking about, but curiosity got the better of her.

She followed them through the doors, bypassing the route to the parking lot.

"And, now we're back on set where we started!" Reed was standing in front of the group. "So, that's pretty much the whole tour. What did you guys think of being on a Hollywood set?"

"I want to be an actor!" one kid shouted out, waving his hand to be seen.

Teagan noticed another girl in a wheelchair pushing her way to the front of the group. "Can we take pictures?" she asked.

"Sure." Reed smiled. "Let me grab the photographer, and we'll get some nice ones with everyone."

"Yay!" the kids cried in unison, all pulling out their cell phones and primping for the camera.

Teagan stayed back, walking along the edge so she was mostly out of sight. She didn't want Reed to see her or to be caught spying on him. *What am I even doing?* She honestly wasn't sure why she was here, or why she found this exchange so fascinating. Maybe it was because she'd been like these kids once, bound to a chair, and seeing them get a chance to meet and take pictures with a man who was clearly their idol? It was heartwarming.

A man walked over with a large camera, and Teagan recognized him as Reed's agent, Jason. He took pictures of each of the children with Reed on set. He even retook the photos with the child's individual cellphone as well. Lastly, they took a group photo all together, and Teagan smiled at the way Reed's arm circled the kids affectionately.

He looked in his element in a way she hadn't seen before. There were still parts of her that felt like she knew everything there was to know about Reed, and maybe at one point that had been true. But watching him now, it was clear that there was a lot more to him than she remembered, or than she'd seen gracing the covers of tabloids over the last few years.

Teagan's jaw tensed when she caught her line of thinking, realizing she was...she was liking him. She was feeling positive, affectionate things toward the man who had left her at the altar. And the worst part was, she didn't want to push those thoughts away. She wanted to embrace them. She wanted to let her walls down and open herself up to the possibility that maybe everything she'd been harboring could finally be let go.

When each child had finished taking their photos and was

escorted away by a parent or guardian, Teagan decided to go up to Reed and compliment him on what he'd done. She approached him, but he was talking to his agent and didn't see her.

"That was great, Reed," Jason said, patting his client on the shoulder.

Reed nodded, apparently still not seeing her. "Did you get the photos you needed for the magazines?"

"Definitely. They're going to love this good guy image."

Teagan blinked, stopping mid-stride. *Good guy image*. It had all been an act. He didn't care one bit about those kids or what they were going through in life. It was a publicity stunt, a little good will for the audience to fix the image he'd created for himself over the last few years.

She felt stupid for believing it could have been anything else.

Turning around, she headed back for the studio door.

"Teagan?" She could hear Reed calling out behind her, but she didn't look at him and she didn't stop walking. A few moments later, he caught up to her anyway. "Teag. I didn't see you there. What are you doing on set on a Saturday?"

She flashed him an annoyed look. "I was practicing. I always do."

"Is something wrong?" He looked confused, but matched her stride as they walked through the set door and headed toward the parking lot. "You sound angrier than usual."

"I'm not angry," she gritted out. "I'm just...I feel foolish."

He looked even more confused now. "Why?"

"Nothing." She sighed and pulled her keys out of her pocket. "Just forget it, okay?"

"Teagan, talk to me. I obviously did something to piss you off."

They reached her car and Teagan opened the driver's side door then paused and turned to look at him. "I don't know who you are anymore, Reed."

He closed the gap between them, his hands on the top of the

car door between them. "Then get to know me. Have dinner with me. Let's talk and catch up on everything we've missed."

She studied his face for a moment, almost considering it. Then she shook her head. "That wouldn't be a good idea."

"Why not?" Reed continued to push, his green eyes sparkling with pain and lust somehow tangled into one. "It doesn't have to mean anything. Just two people who once knew each other, catching up on lost time. It doesn't even have to be dinner. What about lunch, tomorrow?"

Teagan nibbled on the edge of her lip, struggling to find a reason to reject his offer. And honestly, not wanting to. "All right. Lunch tomorrow."

"Text me your address right now and I'll pick you up tomorrow at noon," he instructed. "I'm not taking a chance of you getting cold feet."

She laughed despite her hesitance. "I'm not the one who struggles with cold feet, Reed. You text me the address where we're going and I'll meet you there." She wasn't ready to let him come over to her house, see where she lived, or give him that level of intimacy. Though, honestly, she wasn't sure she trusted herself not to pull him into her apartment and jump him. "I'll see you tomorrow."

"I'm counting down the hours," he said, reaching for her hand and giving it a small squeeze.

When he let go, Teagan climbed back into her car and quickly put it into drive. She needed to put distance between them as soon as possible so she could evaluate what the hell she'd just agreed to and just how dumb she really was.

CHAPTER SEVEN

"TEAGAN!" Aria, her oldest sister, wrapped her arms around Teagan's neck and crushed her into a bear hug. "I've missed you!"

She laughed, hugging her sister back. "It's only been a week since you saw me."

"More like a month." Aria scoffed and let go of her. "You haven't been home to see the folks in a while either. Dad's asking about you and your big movie."

"It's not *my* big movie. I'm just working on it."

Aria shrugged, then reached down and lifted the small young girl who was pulling on her skirt. Cradling her on her hip, she kissed her daughter's forehead. "Tillie, did you say hi to Auntie Teagan?"

Teagan made a silly face at her niece and then gave her a loud, squeaky kissy on her pudgy two-year old cheek. "Hi, baby girl. I missed you!"

"Hi, Tee," Tillie said with a lopsided smile, putting her arms up to be held.

Teagan obliged and swung her young niece into her arms, bouncing her on her hip and singing a nursery rhyme to her.

"Are you sure you don't mind watching her tonight?" Aria asked again, now standing in front of Teagan's mirror and surveying her reflection. She was clearly dressed for a party in a sparkling black cocktail gown and soft white pearls. "I couldn't believe our sitter canceled on us at the last minute. It's not like I can just reschedule Ben's movie premiere. 'Sorry, can't find a sitter, let's do the red carpet another Saturday night?'"

Teagan laughed at her sister's sarcastic tone. "I really don't mind at all. I didn't have any other plans, and I love spending time with Tillie."

"She's my angel." Aria beamed and kissed her daughter's head again. They moved over to Teagan's living room and set Tillie up with a box of toys that Teagan always kept there for her. Of course, Tillie ignored the toys and decided to yank Benson's tail instead—causing him to screech and run out of the room.

Teagan tried not to laugh. "Tillie, be nice to Benson! He's old."

"I literally just called you an angel, babe." Aria collapsed on the couch beside her with a laugh. "Well, I've got a good ten minutes until Ben gets here, so catch me up on your life. I want to know every detail of my baby sister's existence."

Teagan briefly considered lying about her current...situation, but there was no point. Aria was one of the biggest actresses in Hollywood these days, and Ben's reach as a high-level producer was even further. Hell, his company was funding their movie, along with dozens of others. He rarely got down in the day-to-day details, but if they didn't know she was working with Reed by now, they would very soon.

"Um, it's actually a little complicated." Teagan fidgeted with her fingers in her lap.

Aria wiggled her eyebrows. "Those are the best kinds of stories. Spill."

Teagan hesitated for a minute then sighed. "I'm training the lead actor on *Break Down*, choreographing his set list with his costar."

Aria nodded. "The dance film, I know. It's supposed to be huge, I heard! Ben was already telling me about the promotions they've got lined up for the release. It sounds like it's going to be a big hit."

"Did you also hear it's starring Reed Scott?" Teagan glanced up at her sister to gauge her reaction. "As in...*Reed Scott.*"

Aria stared at her for a moment, then recognition hit her eyes and they widened as her mouth fell open. "Reed Scott...like *your* Reed? I mean, I knew he was an actor, but I didn't know he was on your film. He's...wait, what? This is crazy. So, you're working with that asswipe?"

"Yeah..." Teagan chewed on the edge of her lip, still unsure how she felt about it all herself. She'd definitely hated him the moment she saw him, and had completely freaked out over the idea of having to train him. But since then...well, a lot had happened. And tomorrow, they were having lunch. *Catching up.* Whatever that means.

She'd also been watching him filming, and his acting was some of the best she'd seen. He was nothing but a professional on set, even when he was at practice with her and Elena. It was a stark contrast to the Reed Scott she'd seen disgracing the tabloids over the last few years. Her stomach turned at the memory of all the photos of him with other women. She couldn't even go to a damn grocery store without seeing the man she'd almost married taking jello shots off of a stripper's stomach.

But *that* Reed wasn't the man she'd seen on set the last two weeks, and she hoped to God it wasn't him at all. But, in the same moment, she was frustrated she even cared.

"And *you* are the one who has to train him? They can't have another choreographer do it?"

Teagan shook her head adamantly. *Hell no.* "I don't want

anyone else to do it. This is my career—and this job is huge for me. You know how hard I've worked to get back to my career, work my way back up the ladder. I can't throw that away because my ex-fiancé walks in the door."

Aria reached her hand over and squeezed Teagan's. "He isn't just your ex-fiancé, Teag. He left you at the altar. He didn't visit you once in the hospital—a hospital you wouldn't have even been in if you'd been happily married and on your honeymoon." Aria let out a deep breath, leaning back into the couch cushions and closing her eyes. "God, I could just kill him."

"Believe me, so could I." Teagan chuckled lightly, though none of this felt particularly funny. "I'm not going easy on him. I'm not letting him back in. He knows very clearly that I...I hate him."

"Oh, crap." Aria released a dramatic sigh. "You don't hate him. Shit. I can't believe you don't hate him."

"What are you talking about?" Teagan furrowed her brows. "I literally just said I did."

"Yeah, you *said* it, but your face didn't." Aria pointed at Teagan's face and waved her hand around. "The rest of you probably didn't either. You're going to get suckered back in by his charm and fall head over heels again. He's your kryptonite —always was."

Teagan shook her head. "I can promise you a thousand percent that me falling in love with Reed Scott for a second time is absolutely not ever, ever, *ever* going to happen."

Aria looked at her for a minute then rolled her eyes. "Good lord. Just don't tell Mom and Dad."

A knock on her front door interrupted the snappy response Teagan was about to deliver back to her sister.

Aria jumped up to answer it and then greeted her husband, Ben Lawson, with a giant hug and kiss. "Ben, did you know who was starring in *Break Down?*"

Ben wrapped his arm around his wife's waist, pressing a kiss below her ear. "Reed Scott. Why?"

Aria pointed at Teagan. "Did you also know that Reed Scott left Teagan at the altar eight years ago?"

Ben's eyes flamed and he looked between them. "What? *That's* Reed? The actor Reed Scott?" Ben pulled his cell phone out of his pocket and began dialing. "I'll have him removed from the project immediately."

"No!" Teagan put her hands up. "Are you two crazy? I am an adult and perfectly capable of taking care of myself. I do not need my big sister and brother-in-law coming to my rescue."

Aria frowned. "Okay, but if I see him, am I allowed to punch him one time? Just once. I swear, it won't even be that hard. I'm not that strong."

"My punch will be hard," Ben clarified, flexing his bicep and showing off. "Like, knock him to the ground and stomp on him strong."

Teagan couldn't stop the laughter from bubbling up at the absurd images they were creating. She knew they'd never actually do anything aggressive, but she also knew Aria and Ben would do anything for her. They were her family and she loved them with everything in her. "You guys realize your daughter can hear your violent rampage, right?"

Ben smiled and walked over to Tillie, lifting her up with a big, silly roar. "My girl's going to be a badass, right, Til? You going to punch all those boys in the face and never, ever, ever, ever date anyone?"

Tillie squealed and kicked her legs, laughing and falling into her father's arms. "Never!"

Aria kissed Ben's cheek. "You're impossible. Come on, we're going to be late."

Ben handed Tillie to Teagan, and she cuddled right into her

side, laying her head on Teagan's shoulder. "Be good to my girl, Teag. And Til? Don't terrorize your auntie."

"No!" Tillie clapped her hands as she shouted her favorite word.

Ben headed for the door, but Aria lagged behind for a moment. Leaning in closer to Teagan, Aria lowered her voice. "Just be careful, Teagan. No matter who he is now, or what's left between you—don't forget what he cost you."

Teagan nodded, because despite what had happened between her and Reed, her sister was right. And even more so, she wasn't sure it mattered anymore.

CHAPTER EIGHT

REED LOOKED AROUND NERVOUSLY, examining every aspect of the scene he'd just created. It had to be perfect. A red checkered blanket stretched out across the faux grass on set, and on it sat a wicker basket with wine, cheese, and charcuterie. It was arranged in the middle of an outdoor backdrop on set, with a sunrise painted behind them and a fake squirrel sitting a few feet away next to an even faker tree.

Honestly, he wasn't sure what movie this set was used for, but they needed better set designers.

Either way, Teagan had agreed to lunch with him—*to catch up*—and that's exactly what he was going to do. Their very first date in college had been a picnic on the quad on campus, though back then it had been watery beer and some sandwiches he'd nabbed from the cafeteria wrapped in a Ziploc bag.

He was going to reenact every moment of that date, reminding her exactly what they had to catch up on. Reminding her who he was, who *they* were, because he wasn't sure he'd have another chance. The fact that she'd said yes to lunch had been surprising enough.

"Reed?" Her voice floated to him from somewhere behind him.

When he turned to face her, he realized that this was the first time he'd seen her not in leggings and a leotard. She was wearing a loose-fitting pink t-shirt over a dark pair of jeans. Her body was still lithe and breathtaking, even in denim, as she glided across the room to join him.

"When you said you'd text me the address of our lunch date, I hadn't expected it to be at work," she kidded, chuckling and looking around. "What's all this?"

He gestured to the picnic area he'd created with one hand, and took her hand with the other. "We're having a picnic."

Her brows lifted, and a tiny smile appeared at the corner of her lips. "I can't remember the last time I've had one of those."

"I remember my last picnic," he replied, pulling her down onto the checkered blanket. "Twelve years ago... our first date."

Teagan's gaze lifted to his, and she nibbled on the edge of her lip.

"I'm *not* implying anything with this," he quickly clarified. "I just wanted to do something sentimental, to commemorate the moment."

She looked skeptical, her eyes narrowing. "Well, I'm certainly not going to forget this."

He was going to take that as a compliment. "Thank you. Now, would you like some wine?"

"Sure." She lifted the empty wine glass, and he grabbed the already-open bottle from the basket, then poured it in hers first, then his. "Cheers."

They clinked glasses together, then both took a sip. He pulled out the meats and cheeses next, arranging it in front of her.

"This looks delicious," she admitted, spreading some goat cheese on a cracker. "Much better than what we ate on our first date."

"We're not dumb college kids anymore," he teased. "We get better with age."

She didn't say anything to that, and he realized she might be reading more into what he was saying than he meant. *Shit.* Things were awkward. He was trying for a nice moment, but tension hung between them and he had no idea how to fix it.

"So..." she started, clearly feeling as uncomfortable as he was beginning to. "We're here to catch up. Right?"

He nodded. "What's new in your life?"

"In eight years?" She tapped a finger to her bottom lip. "Uh, kind of a lot."

"Well, what about your family?" he suggested, trying to narrow the topic. Fuck, this was strange. Suddenly he couldn't recall why he thought any part of this would be a good idea.

"Aria's married." A smile finally returned to Teagan's face, and she relaxed. "They have a beautiful daughter, Tillie. I babysat her last night."

"That's wonderful," Reed said, though admittedly, he had followed Aria's career somewhat. It was hard not to since they were in the same circles. "I have a niece, too. Nell."

"Penelope had a daughter?" Teagan put a hand over her heart. "That's wonderful. Do you have pictures?"

He pulled out his phone and they traded photos of Nell and Tillie, gushing over each other's nieces. The pride in his voice was evident, because Nell was his life and she had been since she was born six years ago.

"I love the way you talk about her," Teagan said, handing him back his phone. "It makes yesterday feel more...genuine."

He furrowed his brows, unsure what she meant. "Yesterday?"

"The publicity stunt with all those kids." She looked down at her hands fidgeting in her lap. "It was so wonderful what you were doing for them. I *was* really impressed."

"And you're not now?"

She shrugged. "I thought you'd done it out of the goodness of your heart, not to fix your image in the public."

The look on her face yesterday—crestfallen and disappointed —it made sense now. He hated that he'd done that to her, and he hated even more that he couldn't deny it. That was exactly what had happened. She was right.

"I...I don't know how to explain yesterday in way that would make you feel better, or see me differently," he admitted. "It *was* a publicity stunt. My agent wants to fix my image. He wants the public to stop seeing me as the playboy partier the paparazzi has made me out to be." Reed sighed. He was making this worse. "But I can tell you that even though it wasn't my idea, and it wasn't my doing, I really enjoyed yesterday. I loved every minute of being with those kids, and seeing their struggles was...shit, it was inspiring as hell. Those kids have been through more than I've ever been in my entire life, and not one of them looked like it bothered them. They were just happy and living their life, and I admire that kind of strength."

She studied him carefully, as if she was trying to decide what to think or feel about everything he'd just said. "I feel that from you now, honestly. The way you talk about Nell, the way your face lights up...it's genuine. Yesterday, I just...I'm not sure."

"You don't trust me or my motivations," he finished for her. "And that's okay. You have every reason not to trust me."

Teagan's eyes watered slightly, and she swallowed hard, her jaw tensing. She dropped her gaze down to her lap and the glass of wine in her hand. "I spent so many years hating you, Reed." Finally, she raised her head back up to look at him. "It's honestly relieving to let that go. I don't think I even understood what a darkness that was on my heart all this time, but these last two weeks with you, learning the things I have...I feel lighter."

Reed smiled a little, trying to keep his hopes from leaping out of his chest and running to her. Though, it was already too late.

"I'm glad, though I'm so sorry I made you feel that way for so long."

Teagan put down her glass and scooted closer to him on the blanket. "Can I tell you something?"

He nodded.

"I'd already turned down the Broadway role a week before our wedding," she admitted.

His eyes widened. He hadn't known that. Hell, that role had been the entire reason he'd convinced himself he needed to end things with her. "I...I didn't know."

"It was going to be a surprise," she admitted. "Ironic, right?"

Reed felt like his chest was about to cave in from the ache in his heart. God, he wanted to go back and change everything. He wanted to rewrite their story. He wanted to write their epilogue—give them a second chance at finishing what they'd started.

"I don't know what to say, Teag. I feel like you lost so much because of me."

She shook her head. "We're letting go of all of that now. Right? Moving on?"

"I'd like that a lot," he admitted. "But are you sure? I don't deserve it."

"Of course you don't deserve it." She smiled, a teasing glint in her dark brown eyes. "So, it's a good thing life isn't fair."

Reed laughed, pulling her into him for a hug. "Speaking of unfair, I have something to show you."

She lingered pressed against his chest, and he was glad she did because there was something magical about the way she fit in his arms. "What is it?"

He stood and pulled her to her feet beside him. "Come on."

Leading her off the set, he took her in the direction of the dressing rooms. After a few turns down several hallways, he paused in front of a door with an empty slot where the name should be. Reed pulled a key out of his pocket and stuck it in the lock, opening the door and flipping on the light.

"What are we doing in here?" Teagan asked, walking into the dressing room slowly. "Who's is this?"

Reed gestured toward the other end of the room where there was a mirrored wall and a bar. He didn't expect her to actually use it for practice, since there wasn't as much space as the studio, but he'd wanted it put in for her anyway. There was a brightly-lit vanity and counter to one side, and a plush couch and lounge area to the other that even had a mini-fridge he'd made sure was stocked full of her favorite drinks. "It's yours. I had your things transferred."

She knit her brows and stared at him. "What are you talking about?"

"That other room of yours was basically a closet, Teag. Hell, smaller than a closet. You need actual space. Hell, you're on set as much as I am, if not more, and you're one of the hardest working people on staff."

Teagan walked farther into the room, examining everything around her then slowly turned back to face him. "This...this is basically the size of my apartment."

"Well, damn, we should get you a new apartment next."

She laughed and shook her head. "I don't know what to say, Reed."

"Don't say anything." Honestly, he wasn't looking for thanks. He just wanted her to have the space she needed—and deserved. "It was seriously nothing."

"You know you don't need to give me anything, right? I'm not someone whose attention you have to buy."

Reed chuckled. "I'm fully aware of your aversion to all things materialistic. This is more for me than you. Now I don't need to worry about you."

"You were worried..." She furrowed her brow. "About *me*?"

"Well, that closet was way in the back lot, the farthest possible from set. It's nowhere near the security guard shack, and I just..." He rubbed the back of his neck. *Shit, what was he saying?* "I just wanted you closer."

Teagan walked toward him and then past him. She closed the door to the dressing room behind him. Turning back around, Teagan faced him and put her hands square on her hips. "If I do something, can you not read into it? Not think it means something more than it does?"

Huh? "Uh...sure? I don't really know what that means, but—"

She didn't wait for him to finish before she threw her arms around his neck and pressed her lips to his.

Reed's eyes widened, but then he didn't miss a beat either. He wrapped his arms around her back and pulled her body flush to his. She ran her fingers through his hair, and their tongues danced as they tasted one another.

It was everything he remembered kissing Teagan to be, but, somehow, it was so much more. This wasn't the young girl who'd been his college sweetheart. This was a woman who had long outgrown the inhibitions of age. She knew what she wanted, and she knew how to take it from him—and he wanted to give it to her, everything she asked for and more.

His hands slid down her back, scooping under her ass and lifting her against his body. She automatically wrapped her legs around his waist and anchored her arms to his shoulders as their lips continued to crash against one another, hungry and wanting. Walking them over to the vanity, he sat her on the counter and pushed her knees apart.

Reed stepped between her legs, and he knew she could feel his dick pressing against her core even through his pants. After years apart, he needed no time to prepare. His body wanted her—*now*.

Letting his lips fall south, he kissed across her jaw and down her neck. He nibbled and licked a trail to her collarbone, and then across the fleshy mounds of her breast above the hem of her shirt. She moaned, pushing her hips against him and letting her head fall back.

It was by far the sexiest sound he'd ever heard in his life, and his dick practically throbbed as he listened to her pant and gasp with every new sensation. Eager to hear what other sounds she could make, he let his hand slide up her inner thigh and dip inside her jeans. She spread her legs wider, encouraging him on.

"You're soaked," he said, growling roughly in her ear as his fingers found her center.

She moaned again, clutching tighter to his shoulders, her face buried against his neck.

Reed circled his fingers over her swollen clit, loving the way she trembled and shook against him. Pushing farther, he slid two fingers inside her, but kept his thumb rubbing against her clit.

"Ah!" She gasped, thrusting her hips forward with his movements. "Oh, God, I'm close."

His mouth found hers again, and they nipped, kissed, and caressed one another with their lips until her tremors overtook her. Her moans were thick and heavy against his ear, her body clenching around his fingers as he felt her climax power through her body in waves.

When she finally began to quiet against him, he removed his fingers but continued rubbing slow, soft circles against her clit. She jolted every few seconds as the aftershock of her orgasm continued to hit her.

Teagan slid her hand slowly down his chest, still pressed tightly to him. Moving below his belt, she rubbed against his hard dick through his pants and he nearly exploded then and there. She went to undo his belt buckle, but he grabbed her hand and removed it.

"Not yet," he instructed, placing small kisses on her cheek. "I want you to trust me first."

He couldn't believe himself—stopping a hand job? Maybe more? That certainly wasn't his style. But as much as he wanted to slam his dick into her and drain every bit of pleasure he could, he also...didn't. He didn't want to treat her like the other women he'd fucked and forgotten.

Teagan was different. She was so much more, and when they had sex, it would be because she loved him and trusted him again. He wouldn't let her settle for less.

CHAPTER NINE

I'M in way too deep. Teagan watched Reed and Elena dancing together on set, the cameras rolling as he spun her around and dipped her close. They rolled their bodies up to a standing position slowly, her hand on his face as they came close to kissing. The camera panned in on their faces, the way they looked at each other—unsure, but wanting. In love, but terrified.

It was a familiar feeling.

The movie was filming the scene where the main characters first realized they were falling in love, and the chemistry between Reed and Elena was undeniable. Sure, Teagan knew it was just acting—and at that, Reed was insanely talented. But it didn't make the jealousy swirling in her stomach lessen any when he pressed his lips to Elena's.

She kissed him back, gentle and soft. It was nothing like the hungry, needing way Reed had kissed Teagan yesterday.

Her cheeks flushed at the memory of their actions in her new dressing room. She still couldn't believe she'd been so wanton as to kiss him like that. She was surprised at both how far it had gone, and how quickly it had stopped. The fact that he wanted to wait and didn't want to jump into bed...it was relieving. Her libido had definitely taken over, and now that she had had a chance to step back and think it all through, she was realizing how insane it all was.

They were *not* getting back together. Going down this path would only lead to another heartbreak, and that was not something she was interested in anymore. Still...their chemistry. The fire between them when he'd kissed her, when he'd brought her to climax with just his skilled fingers...it felt impossible to deny. Impossible to walk away from.

Ever since yesterday, her body had been in a constant state of arousal. Every thought, every move, all brought her mind back to sex and Reed and how badly she wanted every inch of him. Hell, the way Elena was looking at him right now, it seemed she was feeling the same thing.

Reed broke their kiss, and lovingly stared into Elena's eyes. A small smile lifted the corners of his lips as the camera faded away. God, he was fantastic. Watching them, Teagan could almost believe it was real. If he hadn't been making her come on his hand less than twenty-four hours ago, she might have thought there was more between them.

"Cut!" Mario called out, walking on to the set and Elena and Reed let go of each other. "Fantastic job. I think we got it on that take."

"You were fantastic," Elena agreed, running a hand down Reed's chest. "And a great kisser."

Reed chuckled lightly, though he didn't look uncomfortable. Instead, he was watching Teagan. "Glad we finally got those dance moves down. That one was a hard number."

Teagan gave him a small smile, walking closer.

Elena shrugged her shoulders. "It wasn't that hard. I think the choreography could have been better."

This bitch. Teagan turned her attention away from Reed and looked at Elena. "Was there a problem with my routine?"

"No," Elena said, an unmistakable attitude in her voice. "You have to admit it was a little elementary. We could have handled more." Elena placed her forearm on Reed's shoulder, molding her body to his side. "Reed's very talented...with his body."

"Oh, I'm *very* familiar of his talents," Teagan assured her, trying very hard not to roll her eyes. "But I'll amp up next week's routine for you. Maybe give you a solo dance scene. All. Alone."

Reed glanced between the two women. "Uh..."

Elena's nostrils flared, and she looked between Reed and Teagan. "I'm going to my dressing room." Elena stormed away, flouncing across the set with a stomp in each step.

"Have a lovely day," Teagan called after her, her voice oozing a false sweetness that was not at all professional and not at all like her. Honestly, she'd never had a standoff with another woman over a man before, but that was undeniably what was happening right now.

Over *Reed.*

Teagan was beginning to wonder more and more if she was even capable of walking away at this point, or if she needed to see this out. It was getting harder and harder to see where the line was between who they were eight years ago and who they were now.

"Well, that was awkward." Reed looked at her. "What the hell was that?"

Teagan shrugged. "I don't know what you're talking about."

He stepped closer, leaning in to speak softly into her ear. "If I didn't know better, I'd say you were fighting over me."

"Not everything is about you, Reed," she assured him. She was mostly lying, but he didn't need to know that. "I'm very passionate about my routines, and I don't like them being called elementary."

"Fair. That was a bit rude," he agreed. "Plus, that routine was hard as fuck."

"Thank you."

"Reed!" Mario walked over to them. "Plane's taking off in two hours. Your assistant has everything packed and on board."

Reed nodded. "I'm ready."

They were filming a scene on location in Napa Valley, which was about a two-hour flight from Los Angeles. Teagan's things were already packed and in the back of her car, since she was planning to drive up—though she was definitely not looking forward to the long car ride. Thankfully, her neighbor was feeding Benson for the week, so she didn't have to worry about being away from home for too long.

Mario slapped him on the back. "Great. We're going to knock out those scenes. Teag, how's the choreography for the vineyard?"

"I'm almost done with it, but I think it'll be great. I just need to see the actual set to finish it up."

"Makes sense," Mario said. "When will you arrive at the winery?"

"It's about a six-or-seven-hour drive, so pretty late tonight."

"That's ridiculous," Reed interjected. "Fly with me."

"That would be easier," Mario agreed. "There's plenty of room on the plane. I'll tell my production assistant to get your suitcase on board."

Teagan looked between the two men. Admittedly, flying on a private plane sounded a thousand times better than fighting Los Angeles traffic. "Um, I guess I could do that." She glanced at Reed. "It *would* probably be easier."

"It's settled then." Reed clapped his hands, then stalked away, probably to go find the PA.

Mario looked over at her. "Hey, listen, Teag...this may not really be my place to say, but I think I need to."

She furrowed her brow. "What's wrong?"

"You and Reed—is there more there than working together? Anything I need to be aware of?"

She swallowed hard, unsure what to say. Lying to her boss wasn't something she was in the habit of doing, but she also genuinely didn't know the answer to what was going on with her and Reed. "We, uh, we're not anything right now, if that's what you're asking."

He furrowed his brow. "But?"

"We've been a thing in the past," she admitted. "It didn't end well."

Mario sighed. "That's what I was worried about. Look, I don't have a problem with on-set dating, but I do have a problem if it compromises the work. Elena's already making complaints, and if there's tension, it becomes a problem. Not to mention that Reed's fighting an uphill battle on fixing his image before we premiere. So, just keep all that in mind. These are not low stakes. Millions are on the line."

But no pressure, she thought to herself.

"We're professionals," she assured him. "Reed is a professional."

"Great." With that, Mario walked away.

Teagan wrapped her arms around her own waist and wondered just how badly she was fucking up her life right now, because nothing had even happened between her and Reed, and yet, it was already a mess.

And worse yet? She was excited to be on the plane with him. She was excited to spend a week in Napa Valley with him. She was excited...and that was the last thing she ever thought she'd be feeling about Reed Fucking Scott.

CHAPTER TEN

"WE ARE PREPARING FOR TAKE-OFF," the captain of the plane came over the small loudspeaker and announced to the passengers. "Please take your seats and buckle your seatbelts. You can remove them once we're safely in the air and the seatbelt sign has been turned off."

Teagan looked around at the plush leather arm chairs that the small group of ten or so people were sitting in. The majority of the seats were already taken, but she spotted an empty one facing away from her toward the back of the plane.

Only one problem. It was directly facing Reed.

"Teag," he called out to her. "There's a free seat here." He gestured to the chair across from him as he stood up to let her in.

"Hey, Teagan!" Taylor waved at her as she walked past her chair.

Teagan smiled at her. She and Taylor had struck up quite a friendship during the last few weeks, and she really enjoyed training the young actress. She was a natural dancer, and reminded her a lot of herself at that age. "Hey, Taylor."

She continued walking toward the back of the plane and let

Reed take her bag from her. He tucked it into an overhead compartment as she settled in and pulled her seatbelt across her lap. "Thank you."

When he sat back down, his knees were touching hers from how close they were sitting. There was technically a lot of space, but his legs were so long that he was still practically on top of her. The next closest chair was across the aisle where two production assistants were sitting, busily tapping away on their laptops.

"I've never been on a private plane before," she admitted, looking around in amazement at the luxury and space that commercial planes definitely didn't have. Her chair had a small side table next to it with a cold bottle of water for her. She never thought she'd be so impressed with water, but admittedly, she was a bit star struck by it all. "Do you always fly like this?"

He shook his head. "Definitely not. It was just easier for the movie than coordinating all the different flights and worrying about who's going to make it there on time or not."

"I guess so, but still..."

"Despite most of Hollywood, I swear I'm not some highbrow asshole who flushes cash down the toilet." Reed laughed, and she tried not to notice the way his eyes crinkled at the corners when he was truly happy. "You saw how I grew up. I swear, I'm as grounded as they come."

"Says the man who strong-armed me into a giant dressing room."

Reed smirked, giving her a wink. "I believe the correct phrasing is that I fingered you in a giant dressing room."

Her eyes widened and she her cheeks burned as she looked around to see if anyone had heard him. "What the hell, Reed?"

"Sorry." His eyes glittered. *He isn't sorry.*

"Annnnyways," she emphasized. "I'm just saying, you can't impress me with a dressing room or plane or flashing your money around."

"I'm not trying to impress you." He smiled again, that stupid smirk that both infuriated and turned her on. "We already established that, remember?"

"Right." She rubbed her hand up and down her arm, her cheeks still on fire. "Exactly."

The plane was safely in the air at this point, and she leaned back in her chair and took a sip of her water. Anything to cool her down. Glancing out the small plane window, she watched California gliding by beneath them. It looked so simple and uncrowded from above. As much as she wanted to pretend that her problems could stay below on the ground, they were definitely thirty thousand feet above with her.

Or, more accurately, *he* was with her.

Teagan crossed her legs, tugging her skirt down to ensure her scar was covered. Most of the time, she never thought about it. It was just a part of her. But when people saw it—the pity in their eyes—she couldn't stand that. She didn't want to be defined by her accident, and even more so, she didn't want Reed to see her that way. If he did see it, she'd have to explain why it happened.

She'd have to explain how it was his fault.

Still, she felt guilty for keeping it from him—which was ridiculous. She didn't owe him anything, and even more, she definitely didn't owe him *that* story. Emotions tugged at her heart as she thought about how everything had changed for her that day. If she hadn't had that accident, she might be the star of a dance film, able to toss around money like it was nothing. She might have become a household name, starred on Broadway, or done something else with her life besides help other people find the stardom she'd never have.

Teagan swallowed, pushing the thoughts away. Those dreams were not attainable anymore. While she could dance, and dance well, her physical limitations were still there. She'd accepted that. Period. And, truthfully, she didn't care about money. She was perfectly happy living in her tiny studio apartment with her old, fat cat. As long as she could dance, what more did she need?

"Teag," Reed whispered, rubbing his hand across the outside of her thigh as she blinked her eyes open. "Wake up."

She hadn't even realized she'd dozed off. "I'm awake."

"Follow me," he instructed. "But...in a minute or two."

She furrowed her brow, watching him unbuckle and stand up, walking farther into the back of the plane and disappearing behind a door. Glancing around, she looked at the other members of the production team. Elena was seated toward the front of the plane, fast asleep next to Mario who was talking on his cell phone. The rest of the cast and crew were all doing their own thing and not paying attention.

Quietly, she unbuckled her seatbelt and stood. Trying to make as little noise as possible, she followed in Reed's footsteps and opened the back door, slipping through. Turning around, she realized that they were in a very small bedroom. In fact, the entire room was mostly a bed with a few small shelves around it.

Reed grabbed her the moment she closed the door behind her, wrapping his hand around her wrist and pulling her into his body. His lips were on hers and he kissed her before she even had time to react. His hand cupped her cheek and jaw as he guided her while they kissed, his other hand on her lower back.

She couldn't stop herself from arching into him, her fingers twisting in his shirt as they devoured one another. "Reed." She tried to pause, but she couldn't. She couldn't stop kissing him, or sliding her arms around his neck and collapsing onto the bed beneath him. "Reed..."

"What?" He kissed his way down her neck.

"You said...we can't..." She moaned when he found her favorite spot right below her ear that made her body shiver with desire. "We can't do this."

"We're not," he said against her skin. Reed rested on his

elbows, facing her now and giving them some distance. "I just couldn't sit that close to you any longer without kissing you, Teag. Knowing how good it could be, how good it was...I can't stop myself."

She understood that feeling way more than she wanted to. "Reed...this is going to hurt. We're going to get hurt."

"It already hurts every time I look at you. Every time I remember how badly I screwed everything up." There was a shine in his eyes that almost looked like tears, and a piece of her heart broke open. She could feel her walls crumbling at the intimacy of his admission. "Everything about us hurts, Teag. I've thought about you every single day. I've regretted it every day, as much as I've tried to fix that hole in my heart with every distraction possible. Now you're here, and nothing stops the pain except you being in my arms."

Tears pricked at her lower lashes. "You can't say things like that to me, Reed."

"I can't not say it, either."

"I loved you once. I wanted you—a life with you—forever."

He leaned down and kissed her neck, whispering in her ear, "Why can't we still have that?"

Teagan wrapped her arms around his neck and buried her face against his skin, but she didn't answer. She couldn't. She couldn't tell him because he broke the part of her that believed in everlasting love, that believed love was forever.

She couldn't tell him that she was broken, or that she wasn't sure she'd ever love again. Or that as much as she had spent the last eight years telling herself she deserved better than the man who left her at the altar, that wasn't the truth at all.

Instead, the truth was she was afraid he deserved better than her, than a woman who wasn't whole, who wasn't the woman she'd thought she'd become.

CHAPTER ELEVEN

"I CAN'T DO THIS," Reed said, nearly shouting. "I didn't sign up for any of this!"

Elena stepped toward him. "Jackson, calm down."

"You're part of this, Kelly." He turned away from her, putting his hands on the wooden banister of the deck overlooking the vineyard below. "You're part of them. And me? I have no place in their world. I have no place in yours."

"That's not true." Her hands were on his back, and she placed a kiss against his shoulder. "I refuse to believe that there's any version of this world where we don't belong to each other."

"Your father will never allow it." Reed took Elena in his arms, letting his voice break slightly at the end.

Tears slid down Elena's cheeks. "Jackson, don't you understand by now? I don't care what my father wants. I don't care what any of them want for me. I make my own decisions, and you're who I choose."

He shook his head. "I can't give you the life you're used to, Kel. I can't give you what you deserve. I live in a run-down brick house on the wrong side of town, and I probably always will."

"I don't believe that. You're so talented, Jackson." She pushed up on the tips of her toes and took his face in her hands. "You're going to be a star."

He surveyed her face, carefully looking in her eyes as if he was considering what she was saying. "And if I'm not?"

"Then I'll love your run-down brick house as much as I love you," she whispered.

Reed wrapped his arms around her back and kissed her hard. She leaned her body into his and gasped softly at the motion.

The cameras slowly began to pull back and the sound boom above them followed suit.

"Cut!" Mario called after another minute of their kiss. "Fucking hell, guys. That was amazing." Mario turned to the cameraman beside him. "Could you feel that?"

"Hot," the cameraman agreed.

"The audience is going to be in fucking tears," Mario confirmed.

Reed let go of Elena and smiled at his director. "It felt good. I was really in it."

"Me, too," Elena cooed beside him, wrapping her arm around his.

He shook her off as nicely as possible and walked away to get some water. There was no mistaking Elena wanted more from him, but he had zero interest in anything romantic with her unless it was with a camera pointed at them.

Being on camera made him feel alive in a way he'd never found elsewhere. Getting into character and bringing emotion to a scene gave him a thrill, an excitement, that he'd felt ever since the very first time he'd acted in a play in high school. It just came to him naturally, and he couldn't deny that this is what he was meant to do.

Being on stage, on set, it was his calling.

He didn't necessarily like it when he had to do love scenes or kiss actresses. Or at least, he didn't like it anymore. All he could think about in those scenes was Teagan, and he'd pretend he was talking to her, kissing her, falling in love with her. Though, the truth? He already was.

The more he'd tried to deny it over the last few weeks, the more he'd realized how wrong he was. He'd been so deeply in love with Teagan in college, and despite the distance between them over the last eight years, he'd never stopped. He was still as in love with her today as he'd ever been, maybe even more.

He'd been honest when he'd told her two days ago on the plane that he wanted to try again. He wanted forever. Seeing the tears in her eyes, the strain of agony in her voice...it was devastating. He hated that he'd been the one to hurt her so much, or that he was still hurting her.

But he'd meant what he'd said—he couldn't stay away. He couldn't stop when it was so clear who they were meant to be, what they were meant to be.

A scream suddenly pierced through the air.

Reed whirled around, along with the entire cast and crew.

"Fucking hell." Mario took off on a run toward the scream to the side of the deck they'd just been filming on.

Reed was only a quick step behind him. "What happened?"

When they got to the top of the stairs that led down into the vineyard, Reed saw Taylor laying at the bottom, clutching her ankle. *Fuck.*

Mario was already down at her side, assessing the damage. "Can you move it?" He tried to help her stand, but she screamed and shook her head. "Okay, so that's a no."

"I can't," she cried, tears pouring down her face. "Oh, God, I will just die if it's broken."

"Let's get you to the medic," Mario instructed, already talking into his comm, announcing the injury and calling personnel to the medic tent.

Reed quickly came to her side and helped her stand on her good foot, wrapping one arm around her waist as she clutched his shoulders. "It's not broken. You're going to be fine."

She hopped a few feet then paused, groaning. "I can't."

"I got you," Reed assured her. Leaning down, he swept her up into his arms and carried her the rest of the way to the medical tent in the parking lot of the winery.

Teagan suddenly appeared by their side, walking with them toward the tent. "Taylor, I just heard! Are you okay?"

"Not great," Taylor admitted. "I think I broke my ankle. Though hopefully it's just a bad sprain."

Teagan looked even more upset than Taylor was, as if this somehow personally impacted her or reminded her of...he wasn't sure what. Reed wondered what she was thinking.

Taylor was still whimpering from the pain. "Teag, can you call Jenny?"

"Sure," she agreed. "I'm sure she'll come right up to be with you."

"My wife worries about everything." Taylor sighed. "This certainly won't help things."

Reed carefully placed her on the exam table, and a doctor quickly moved between them. He stepped back and let the medical personnel get to work.

"I'm going to go get my phone," Teagan said, quickly turning back around and heading out of the tent. He followed her, wondering what this would mean for filming.

Reed found Mario over in the main office, which the winery had allowed them to completely take over for the week. Hell, they were paying enough for the location that even though they were closed all week, they were probably still making more than they'd have made on their own.

"Taylor's being seen by medics now," Reed informed the director. "Are we pausing filming?"

"We're going to continue filming today, but only the scenes Taylor isn't in." Mario put his ear piece back in, tuning his comm. "We'll reevaluate once the doctor tells us the verdict."

"Reevaluate?"

Mario looked grave. "If she can't continue, we'll have to reshoot her scenes with another actress."

Reed swallowed hard, hoping that wasn't the case. Taylor was one of the sweetest people on set, and she really deserved to be there. Even more so, she was a social media super star and would be a great asset to the film's publicity when release came.

"Do we even have someone lined up?"

"Nope. And we're on location. Let's hope none of that happens," Mario finished. "Come on, let's get going on the next scene. The vineyard one."

Nodding his head, Reed headed toward the costume department to change into the outfit he'd need for the love scene they were about to film in the vineyard. It was supposed to be one of the most passionate scenes of the movie—almost literally having sex in the middle of rows and rows of grapes.

Honestly, he wasn't sure he'd be able to get his head into it. Sex scenes were always awkward, and even though he'd be mostly clothed in this one, it was still going to be a weird experience. Especially with Elena, because the more and more they continued filming, the more flirtatious she became. He was careful not to give her the impression he was into it, but that didn't seem to give her pause. Rolling around in the grass beneath grape vines certainly wasn't going to calm things down between them either.

The crew handed him his outfit and he quickly changed into it. Hair and makeup came over next and finished off his look. Teagan was standing off to the side, watching him, when he finally noticed her. "Hey."

She smiled at him. "Hey."

"Everything okay?" He walked over and ran his hand down her upper arm.

Teagan nodded. "I just wanted to say thank you for helping Taylor. That was really sweet of you."

He shrugged his shoulders. "No big deal."

"Paparazzi definitely got a photo of you carrying her," she warned. "Just a heads up."

Reed groaned and rubbed his hand over the back of his neck. "I swear, I never even see those fuckers."

"Hiding is part of their job," she replied. The comm anchored to her belt squeaked out some static, then Mario's voice crackled through.

"Teagan, report to the office please. Teagan to the office."

She turned off the comm and took his hand, pulling him into a corner of the makeup tent that wasn't visible to everyone else. Pushing up on her toes, she wrapped her arms around his neck and kissed him.

Reed moaned against her lips, holding her tightly. It wasn't like their kisses before, which had always been hungry and forceful and so full of need. This was soft and sweet, almost— dare he get his hopes up—loving.

She cradled his face in her hands, then finally released him. "I should probably go."

"If you have to," he said, kissing her softly once more.

Teagan smiled. "Bye, Reed."

"Bye, Teag." She left him standing there, watching her walk away. Everything inside him was warning him to stop, to stay away, to not let himself think that was anything more than what it was. And yet, his heart was already leaping, hoping, wanting it to mean so much more.

CHAPTER TWELVE

"THIS IS A GODDAMN DISASTER," Mario said, tapping the office desk with the back of his pen. "We'll need to reshoot all her scenes. We need to find another actress who can not only dance, but can learn all the routines in less than a day." He groaned. "Oh, and who's close by because we're a fucking six-hour drive from Los Angeles."

Reed shook his head. "There's no way we're going to find someone to take Taylor's role. Can't filming wait until after her surgery?"

The doctor had said she'd pulled a ligament in her ankle, and it needed surgery if she wanted to ever be able to dance again. The recovery time was months, and when it came to filming a major motion picture, that was an eternity.

"We'd lose hundreds of thousands of dollars," Mario replied. "Not an option. I'll call the exec, Ben Lawson, and see what he says, but I guarantee you he's going to say to replace her. It's cheaper to reshoot her scenes than to wait."

"Well, how can I help?" Reed still wasn't sure why Mario

called him in here, because it wasn't often he dealt with studio executive issues. "What can I do?"

"I was hoping you'd have some suggestions—other dancers, actresses, someone you know?" Mario asked. "You've been seen with a shit ton of actresses, so surely you can give one of them a call up and they'll drop everything for you."

Reed laughed. "I don't have a little black book that I can use to go around calling in favors."

"Fuck." Mario sighed, pulling out his cell phone. "All right, I'll call the casting agent."

"Wait!" An idea suddenly popped into his mind that was so obvious he couldn't believe he hadn't said it from the start. "Teagan. Cast Teagan in Taylor's role."

Mario furrowed his brow. "Teagan's a choreographer, not an actress."

"Think about it—she already knows the routine, because she created it. I know for a fact she can act, because she did it in college. I've seen her, and she's good," Reed assured him. "Though dancing is where her passion is, she can do this."

"She does already know the routine..." Mario contemplated the suggestion. "She's gorgeous—and she's here."

"Honestly, she'd be the perfect fit," Reed continued. "It's not a huge role, so there's not a ton of lines to remember, but I know she can do it."

"All right. Let's do a screen test. I'll get her a script and a couple hours to memorize it, then we'll shoot it and see how she does."

Reed nodded. "I'll let her know."

"Sure." Mario waved his hand, as if to say the subject matter was settled.

Reed stood and headed out of the office in search of Teagan. After a good thirty minutes trying to locate her, he finally found her at the top of the hill overlooking the vineyard. She was sitting stoically on a yoga mat, her hands on her knees and her eyes closed.

"Teag?"

She blinked her eyes open. "Hey. What are you doing all the way up here?"

"I could ask you the same thing." He chuckled. "It took me forever to find you."

"Needed a little peace and quiet," she replied. "A little meditation is good for the soul. Come, sit." She patted the grass next to her mat.

Obliging her request, he sat down next to her and stretched his legs out in front of him. "It's a nice view, that's for sure."

"Gorgeous," she agreed. "But you didn't come here for the grapes."

"No," he started, wondering how she'd take the news. Most people would probably be overjoyed and ecstatic for a break like this, but he knew Teagan. She wasn't going to take the news of replacing her friend well. "I wanted to talk to you about something."

She turned her body to face him, stretching her legs out as well. "Okay, shoot."

"They're offering you Taylor's role. She isn't going to be able to complete filming."

Teagan narrowed her eyes. "What?"

"She needs surgery, and the recovery time is too long. The studio wants to replace her, and I suggested they give it to you."

She reached out and smacked him on the shoulder. "What would you do something as stupid as that?"

"Hey!" He rubbed his arm, chuckling. "This is good news for you, you know."

"Oh, yeah, sure. It's great news that one of my friends is so hurt, she's going to lose her job."

"Obviously not that part," he replied. "But there's nothing

either of us can do about that. The role is open and you're perfect for it. You already know her routine, and all you'd have to do is learn a few lines. They want to do a screen test tonight."

Teagan pushed up to her feet and shook her head. "Nope. Not doing it." She began rolling up her yoga mat. "I'm not an actress anymore, Reed. I'm not even a dancer. I'm a *teacher*. That's it."

"We both know that's not true. I saw you in dozens of plays and indie productions in college. You're a great actress." Reed grabbed her hand and stopped her. "And you're by far the best dancer I know. You should be on a stage."

She kept her eyes down, refusing to look at him. "I'm not at that level anymore, Reed. I'm a behind-the-camera person. Okay?"

"Not okay," he shot back. "You'd be amazing at this, Teag."

"I can't do it," she repeated, letting go of his hand and tucking her yoga mat under her arm. "Not anymore."

"I don't understand," Reed said, his volume raising slightly. "You had such drive back in college. You wanted to be on any stage that would book you. You wanted to be famous, not helping others become famous. This isn't the Teagan I know."

She turned on her heel and narrowed her eyes. "You *don't* know me anymore, Reed. That's the whole point. You want to know why?" She was practically yelling now. Then, she grabbed the top of her yoga pants and shimmied them down her legs, stepping out of them entirely.

"What are you doing..." He glanced around to make sure they were alone, since apparently stripping was part of this conversation now.

"Look." Teagan pointed down at her leg and ran her finger across a long scar that stretched from her hip to her knee. "I was in a car accident. I couldn't walk for almost a year. Couldn't dance for another two after that. It took me years to get to where I am now, and I'm damn proud of myself. But, there's always going to be things I can't do. Being a serious dancer? Being on camera? Those are things that are forever out of my reach now."

He blinked slowly, trying to wrap his mind around everything she was telling him. All he could think about is how long she spent suffering, chained to a bed, or a chair, and he hadn't been there. He'd been off filming movies and fucking fans and had never once taken a moment to check up on how she was doing. "I...I didn't know."

"I didn't tell you," she stated matter-of-factly. "But that's the truth. So, I can't do this."

No. He wasn't letting her off that easy. He might need a damn second to process everything he'd just learned, but he wasn't about to let her walk away from this opportunity. "Well, it's fucking stupid."

"Excuse me?" Her expression was taken aback, her hand on her chest. "What did you just say?"

"The fact that you think that accident means you can never be on stage, never be a star—it's fucking stupid." Reed stepped closer to her again. "I've seen you dance. I've seen you act. I know with every fiber of my being that you can do this role if you want it. So, *that's* the question. Do you want it?"

She tensed her jaw, gritting her teeth. Finally, she licked her lips and took a deep breath. "Of course I want it."

He shrugged. "Then it is that simple."

She shook her head for the millionth time. "It's not. Just because I want it doesn't mean I can do it."

"Do you think I know what I'm doing on set? Do you think I'm good at my job?" Reed asked.

Slowly, she nodded. "You're great at what you do."

He took her hands in his. "Then trust me when I tell you I know you can do this."

Teagan let her gaze finally reach his, her eyes lined with tears. "Reed..."

He slid an arm around her waist and pulled her flush to him, kissing her softly. She kissed him back, hungrier than he'd expected. She dropped her yoga mat to the ground and threw her arms around his neck, completely ignoring the fact that she wasn't wearing pants.

He dipped her backwards slightly, kissing down her neck and bringing his lips to her ears. "You can do this, Teag. I'll help you. But there's no part of me that doubts you, not for a second."

He heard her sniffing, her grip on his neck tightening slightly. "Okay," she whispered. "I trust you."

His heart leapt in his chest. "You do?"

She nodded her head, pulling slightly apart to look at him.

"Teagan..." he began, unsure of what to say, or how to thank her for giving him a gift like that. "Are we doing this?"

"I think so," she admitted, her hands on his chest. "I think...I think I can try again."

He grabbed her face and kissed her hard. "Thank God."

She laughed lightly, twisting her hands in his shirt. She slid her hands down to the bottom hem of his shirt and began pushing it up his chest. "Another perk about being completely alone out in the middle of nowhere..."

Reed growled and pulled his shirt the rest of the way off. He gripped her waist and slid her right down to the grass beneath him, climbing between her bare legs. She anchored her knees to either side of his hips. He quickly took off her shirt next, then unbuckled his jeans.

Her lips were back on his, and he nipped her bottom lip before letting his tongue dance with hers. She moaned against his mouth, and every part of him burned with desire at the sound of her pleasure. He pushed his pants down farther, letting himself spring free. She gripped him and slid her hand up and down the length of his shaft.

"Fuck," he groaned, nearly ready to burst just from the feeling of her touching him. He placed small kisses down her neck until he got to the top of her bra. Pushing it down, he let her breast spring free and took her nipple between his teeth.

Her back arched off the grass, and she gasped, pushing her hips against his. She continued to pump her hand against his dick as he sucked and licked her nipples until she was nearly shaking.

"I can't wait," she said, gasping. She pulled him toward her core, but he stopped her.

"I don't have a condom," he admitted. Of all things to cock-block him right now. "I didn't think to bring one."

"Ugh." She groaned, this time with displeasure. "It's my turn to take care of you then."

He lifted one brow, loving the sound of that. "Is that so?"

She pushed at his chest, flipping them over until he was laying in the grass and she was on top of him. She kissed him slowly, then worked her way down his body until she was between his legs. Her tongue slid over the top of his dick, and he nearly came then and there. When she took him into her mouth, it was every bit the bliss he'd remembered it to be. He pumped his hips against her as she sucked and licked him until he was certain he couldn't stand another moment of it.

"I'm going to come," he warned, barely able to hold back. His hands twisted in her hair, but she didn't pull away. Instead, she moved faster and harder until he came, the wave of his climax coursing through his entire body.

He gasped for air as he fell back onto the grass, trying to come down from the amazing high she'd just given him. "Shit, Teag... that was amazing."

It was even better than he'd remembered. She'd definitely grown up since the last time they'd been together, and her confidence was incredibly sexy. She knew what she was doing, and wasn't shy at all. He loved this new side of the Teagan. He loved who'd she become in more ways than one.

Teagan straddled him, smiling and looking proud of herself, but there was no chance he was letting her off without getting her off. He reached between their bodies and placed his thumb against her clit, rubbing circles against her. "Mmm..." She moaned and dipped forward, her eyes closing as she bit her bottom lip.

He used his free hand to play with her nipples until she began to tremble against him. Hooking a finger inside her, and then two, he continued to rub her clit with his thumb.

"Oh, God..." She moved her hips against him, and his dick returned to life at the movement. Damn, he wished he'd brought a condom. Within seconds, she fell apart and collapsed on top of him, then slid to his side, resting her head on his chest. Reed kissed her neck, wrapping his arm around her back.

Suddenly, Teagan sat up and quickly began pulling on her clothes. "Shit!"

"What?" He reached for his shirt and pulled it on. "What's wrong?"

"I've got lines to learn!"

Reed laughed and handed over her shirt as he stood. "Go study, co-star. We've got scenes to film."

She scrambled to her feet, fully dressed, and picked up her yoga mat. Turning back to face him, she quickly ran back and kissed him smack on the lips. "Thank you, Reed. I'm...just, thank you."

He kissed her back. "You earned this."

Teagan smiled, the corners of her eyes crinkling with a mischievous look. "Maybe I finally did."

CHAPTER THIRTEEN

TEAGAN INHALED SLOWLY, trying to find her center. Trying to find any place of peace when all she felt was anxiety. Nerves tumbled through her as her stomach somersaulted.

"Ready?" Mario called out from off stage, slightly behind the cameraman. "We're starting from the top of page forty-seven."

She nodded, glancing right at where Reed and Elena were standing. Their arms were linked and they were posed, ready to begin the group dance number. There were six people on set, and each had a part to play in the intricate dance Teagan had choreographed for the vineyard.

She'd never for a second thought she'd be one of the dancers doing it.

Reed glanced over at her, catching her eye. He winked.

The nerves in her belly slowed, and the smiled, despite herself. His confidence in her had a calming effect, and as she thought about it, she realized that she should be the least nervous one on this set. She'd practiced this routine dozens of times while she was creating it. She knew it better than anyone.

Mario signaled the entire set. "Action!"

Teagan pressed forward on her toes, taking care to stay on her mark. Music suddenly filled the air, and they were off. Waiting for her partner to make his move, she shook her shoulders in rhythm to the beat. He stretched out one arm toward her—a tall, beefy young man who she'd enjoyed training because he was certainly talented. Unfortunately, he was also incredibly dimwitted and couldn't hold a simple conversation without staring down her shirt.

She took his hand and let him twirl her into his chest, pretending to swoon as she kicked up her legs to rest on his thigh. He balanced her there for a moment, and then with the beat, she pretended to fall to the floor.

Excitement pounded in Teagan's chest with every movement, every turn, every placement of her foot. It was all a dance she'd done before in practice, but there was something exponentially different about being on stage...on camera. There was a fire inside her that felt like it'd been put out for so long and was finally roaring back to life.

Her back on the vineyard's dirt ground, she kicked up her legs in time to the other female dancers doing the same thing. They moved in rhythm together, each leg perfectly coordinated as they circled in tangent.

She could see Elena's feet moving with hers, and spotted Reed performing his solo routine perfectly. Pride welled inside her that not only was he so talented, but that those were *her* moves. And now she was beside him, sharing the stage with the man she...liked a lot.

It felt like they were doing this together, and somehow that made it seem even more special than she already felt.

Popping back up to her feet, Teagan leaped into her partner's arms and let him swing her around his body until they landed, faces inches apart and staring at one another as the music came to a close. Their chests were heaving with the extreme workout of the dance, and it looked like they were seconds away from kissing one another.

"And scene!" Mario yelled out. "Damn. I really believed you all wanted to fuck each other just then."

Teagan glanced over at Reed. Elena's hand was on his face, and her lips inches from his. Damn, they really did look like they were about to make out. She took a deep breath, exhaling it forcefully in an attempt to push away the thoughts of jealousy. It took her reminding herself sometimes to remember that he was only acting.

Despite not liking that image, Teagan couldn't put a damper on the pride she was feeling at her first performance. Her smile seemed permanently plastered to her lips, and she, very literally, felt like she was dancing on air. Years and years of physical therapy had left her thinking that this was never going to happen for her—that it wasn't possible.

But here she was, doing the impossible. And it felt freaking amazing.

Reed stepped backward, clapping his hands. "I think that's the best one we've filmed yet." He looked over at Teagan, giving her a wicked grin.

Her stomach somersaulted again, but for an entirely different reason. She began walking toward him, wanting to congratulate him on how well he'd done.

Elena suddenly tossed her arms around his neck and hopped into his embrace, her legs wrapping around his back. He grabbed her, mainly to keep her from falling over, but looked startled. "Reed, you were fantastic!" She placed a big kiss on his cheek and wiggled her hips.

Reed held her waist and removed her from his body like he was unpeeling sticky Velcro. "Uh, thanks."

She pouted then grinned as she was back on her own two feet

again. "Want to go grab some wine? Get in the mood for our next scene together?"

"Actually, he already has plans," Teagan interrupted, sliding her hand into Reed's. His fingers automatically intertwined with hers, and she gave Elena the bitchiest look she could muster up.

"I think Reed can talk for himself, don't you?" Elena cooed in as cutesy of a voice as possible.

Reed looked uncomfortable, but smiled at Teagan. "Actually, Teag can talk for me anytime she wants. I'd follow her around like a puppy dog if she'd let me."

"Oh." Elena looked confused at that answer. "Well, you know where my trailer is. Give my door a knock if you change your mind."

Reed stepped closer to the blonde starlet, lowering his voice. "Elena, I think it's best if we just keep things professional."

Teagan loved the way he not only clarified his boundaries, but did it quietly so as to not embarrass Elena. Granted, Teagan was fine with Elena being embarrassed, but she loved his compassion. It was a side of him she hadn't seen until recently, and she found herself captivated by all these new sides to him.

"Yeah, of course," Elena murmured, ducking her head. "I'd never think otherwise. I was just being friendly." She walked away quickly, leaving them alone on set.

Reed took Teagan's hand again, lifting it to his lips and kissing the back. "Was that jealousy, Ms. Reynolds?"

Her cheeks flushed with heat. "I don't know what you're talking about."

"Is that so?" Reed lifted one brow, stepping closer to her and leaning in to whisper in her ear. "When I saw you dancing—pressed against that other man—I was jealous as hell."

Teagan's tongue slid across her lower lip, her breath quickening. "Maybe I was pretending he was you..."

Reed growled underneath his breath, his eyes fiery. "If we weren't about to start filming the next scene in five minutes, I'd be taking you right back to my trailer."

Teagan laughed, winking at him. "Promises, promises."

CHAPTER FOURTEEN

"Ow!" Teagan blinked her eyes open and looked for the source of the pain on her stomach. Benson was standing square on her stomach, kneading his claws directly into her skin with only the thin bedsheet between them. "Get off, B." She pushed him onto the mattress. "I love you, too, but those claws...ugh."

Benson meowed in complaint and then walked to the end of the bed, turned around a few times, then laid down and fell asleep immediately. *Simple creatures.*

Teagan yawned and climbed out of bed, stretching her limbs. The last week had been one of the busiest of her life—traveling, learning lines, filming, dancing, training others to dance. She was basically doing multiple jobs at the same time, but as physically and mentally demanding as it all was, she couldn't remember a time she'd ever been happier.

Surprisingly, that happiness had nothing to do with Reed either. She was pretty proud of that. She'd found joy in her work, her ambitions, and seeing a future for herself that for so long she hadn't thought was possible. Sure, Reed had been the catapult that brought her this break, but she had spent years earning it with her work ethic and success all on her own.

Reed had assured her of that, and helped her to believe in herself. It was one of the many reasons why she'd opened up her life to him again, and maybe soon, her heart.

Teagan headed to the bathroom and began brushing her teeth, staring at herself in the mirror. She was still terrified to let down those final walls, and even more terrified to tell her family she might possibly be dating her ex-fiancé again. But, in the same vein, she was excited and eager for him to prove her wrong—to prove he could be the man she'd once thought he was.

After their tryst on the hill above the vineyard, they'd kept things pretty tame out of pure necessity. She'd been absolutely exhausted every night when filming wrapped and she'd practiced the choreography for the next day. As much as she'd wanted to fool around, she literally hadn't been able to keep her eyes open.

Reed hadn't minded one bit, and when she passed out the moment she hit the sheets, he just held her all night. They spooned and cuddled, and when she woke up to his bare chest against her, his strong arms around her, she couldn't think of any place she'd rather be.

Teagan rinsed out her mouth and washed her face, then hurried to get dressed. Despite having arrived home late last night, she was still expected to be on set early this morning to continue choreography for the scenes they were filming this week. Reed had even booked her for an early afternoon session and swore he really needed her help.

She'd been sure he was ready for this week's routine, but she wasn't about to complain. Dancing with him was basically her porn.

Finally dressed, Teagan kissed Benson goodbye and headed for her car. Not much later, she was arriving on set and heading straight for the studio. With back-to-back training sessions with cast members, and then filming a quick scene her character was in, Teagan stumbled into her lunch hour, exhausted and starving. Getting back in her car, she headed for one of her favorite sandwich shops a few minutes away.

Within twenty minutes, she was seated and scarfing down her sandwich like it was the last meal she'd ever eat.

"Hey, Teag!" Simone, her youngest sister, waved to her from the other side of the shop. She came over to join her at her table. "Funny seeing you here."

Teagan gave her baby sister a hug, though she was hardly a baby anymore. Simone was attending the University of Southern California and looked as grown up as ever. She had thick black hair, though the entire underside was dyed blue and only visible at certain angles. Simone plopped down into the chair across from her and grabbed the pickle off Teagan's plate, taking a bite.

"So, how are you doing?" She crunched on the pickle. "Mom's been asking why you're not coming over lately."

"I'm not avoiding you guys. It's just insanely busy at work."

"That's what Aria says," Simone teased. "She left yesterday to shoot her new political movie."

"*Dreamers?*"

Simone nodded. "It's already getting Oscar buzz and they haven't even filmed it yet."

"She deserves it," Teagan admitted. "I can't believe she got screwed over for Murals."

"Right?" Simone scoffed. "She definitely should have won for that role. She did win a shit ton of other awards for that one, though. Her career blew up."

"True, but I think she's going to finally get the Oscar on *Dreamers.*" There was no one who deserved it more than Aria. She'd taken her loss in stride, and not once did she even see it as a setback. She just kept going, kept working, and kept fighting for the causes she believed in. Actually, Simone and Teagan both worked on her nonprofit for female empowerment, though she spent the most time and energy on it out of all of them. "How's school, Simmy?"

A staff member came over and deposited a plate bearing a delicious looking sandwich on it in front of Simone; she must have ordered it earlier.

"School's good. I should be graduating next year if everything goes according to plan."

"What about your singing?" Teagan asked. Aria had always been the actress, Teagan was the dancer, but Simone...man, she had the vocals of an angel on her.

"I've got a gig at a dive bar on Friday. So, there's that."

Teagan chuckled. "Well, you've got to start somewhere."

"I'm considering trying out for *The Voice* next year..." Simone took a bite of her sandwich, her expression apprehensive. "I don't know if I'm ready yet though."

"You're definitely ready," Teagan assured her. "Plus, all you promised Mom is that you'd get your degree. After that, your career is all you. You've got to plan ahead."

"Yeah, yeah, yeah." Simone rolled her eyes. "Can you not older-sister me for one lunch? I get enough of that from Aria and Mom."

Teagan smirked and shook her head. "Can't help myself, but if you want, I could tell you some news."

"Ooh, yes. Spill."

"You can't tell anyone else, though," Teagan warned. She knew it was safe to tell her younger sister about Reed, because she had been so young when Reed had left. She wouldn't judge since she had never really been fully there throughout it all. "I'm not ready for the family to know yet."

Simone put down her sandwich and leaned forward against the table. "Okay, now I'm really interested."

"I'm..." Teagan took in a deep breath. "I'm dating Reed...again."

Her sister's brows furrowed, like she was trying to place the name. "Who? Wait...your Reed? Reed, the ex-fiancé?"

She nodded. "One and the same."

"Oh, Mom's going to flip the fuck out." Simone burst out laughing. "Can I be there when you tell her? Please? That can be my Christmas gift."

Teagan balled her napkin and tossed it at her sister. "Come on! Be on my side here."

"I am!" Simone batted away her napkin attack. "Tell me about him. Tell me why on God's Green Earth you'd consider dating him again."

"It happened kind of slowly, to be honest," she explained. "He's the lead on the movie I'm filming, and I've been training him. Now I'm co-starring in a smaller role alongside him. Working together, I've gotten to know who he is now and how he's changed. He's not the same man from back then, and I'm not the same woman."

"That sounds like a line," Simone said, returning to her sandwich. "Everyone changes, but that doesn't mean you can forgive and forget the past."

"I can forgive. I *have* forgiven him." And for the most part, that was true.

"What about for the accident?" Simone pushed. "You've forgiven him for that?"

"That wasn't his fault, Simone."

"It's as much his fault as the car that hit you."

Teagan tried not to think about it. She couldn't change her past, or what she'd been through. And, honestly, she didn't want to blame anyone for that car accident—not even the poor woman who'd hit her car and been devastated by what she'd done. Life was just shit sometimes, and people learned how to shovel it or were buried in it.

"I haven't talked to him about that part of my life yet, or at least, not how he was involved in it," Teagan admitted. "It's just..."

"A looming disaster?" Simone finished for her. "I mean, if he likes you, he's going to be devastated."

Teagan chewed on the inside of her cheek, trying not to think about how that conversation would go. "He's a good guy, Simmy. He made a mistake, and he's trying to amend for that. He's not the same person."

"Well, for your sake, I hope that's true." Simone reached across and squeezed her hand. "If you like him, then I like him."

"I do really like him...a lot," Teagan admitted. "Honestly, I'm trying to hold back, be careful, but...it feels right. He was my other half once, and I think he still is. I think he was always going to be."

Simone put her hand over her heart. "Oh, my God, don't make me cry, Teag."

"Stop!" Teagan laughed.

"You stop," her sister replied, shaking a finger at her. "You're a smitten kitten."

Teagan shrugged one shoulder, trying to hide her smile. "Maybe a little."

Maybe a lot.

CHAPTER FIFTEEN

"REED?" Teagan called out, entering the studio after lunch. She was running a few minutes late and expected him to beat her there for his lesson, but he was nowhere to be seen. Taking a moment to breathe, she placed her bag on the shelf and began stretching.

As busy as her day had been, she'd actually gotten a good night's sleep last night, and it had her thinking about *sleeping* with Reed. She was more than ready to take that step, and, honestly, she'd even do it right here in the studio. She licked her lips at the thought of being pressed up against the mirrored wall, Reed burying himself inside of her.

Good Lord, the things this man did to her mind.

"Hey, Teag." Reed walked into the studio a second later. "I want to introduce you to someone."

Teagan's gaze turned down to the young girl by his side, her hand in his. She immediately recognized her from the pictures he'd shown her of his niece, and quickly rerouted her thoughts to something a little more PG. "Hi, guys! Who's this?"

"This is your student today—Nell." Reed gently pushed his

niece forward, though she looked nervous and was clinging to him. "Nell, this is my really, *really* good friend, Teagan."

Teagan tried not to laugh at his description of her. To be fair, she wouldn't know what to call them either. Friends seemed like the safest explanation, especially in front of a six-year-old. "Hi, Nell. It's wonderful to meet you. Your uncle talks about you all the time."

The little girl smiled up at Reed then shyly stepped forward. Uneven pigtails sat on her shoulders, and she was wearing a plaid dress over stockings that didn't match at all. She put out a pudgy hand and Teagan shook it very stoically, as if they were professionals about to go into a meeting. "Nice to meet you, Teagan."

"Tell her why we're here," Reed encouraged, his hands on her shoulders leading her forward.

Nell grinned, shuffling her feet and picking at a flower on her dress. "We're going to a dance!"

"You're going to a dance?" Teagan gasped, purposefully dramatic. "What dance?"

"Um..." The little girl seemed to consider the question for a minute. "It's for first graders, like me. Only daddy's and daughters, but they said Uncle Reed could be my dad this time because my dad's not here. Mom said it was okay."

Teagan glanced up at Reed, his expression was sheepish.

"Uh, she means it's a Daddy/Daughter Dance. My brother-in-law is deployed, so I'm helping out, going in his place." He rubbed a hand over the back of his neck. "It's not a big deal, but I figured we could get some dance lessons beforehand. Nell wanted to practice."

"Yeah, I want to practice," Nell spoke up. "Addison said I'm a bad dancer and she's going to laugh at me. I don't want those girls to laugh at me, and Uncle Reed said he wouldn't let that happen."

"All right, we don't need to tell her every single thing, Nell," Reed said, looking completely embarrassed now.

He didn't have to be, however, because Teagan was infatuated by the entire scene. She had to take a second to force herself not to cry right then and there, because it was all so heartwarming.

But then she saw Reed's hand when he took Nell's hand in his.

His fingernails were bright pink and glittery, and matched the nail polish on Nell's tiny fingers, too. It was clear she'd painted them on him, because the lines were messy and it honestly looked terrible. But he didn't even seem to notice, and definitely didn't seem to care.

Whatever parts of her heart she'd been holding back from him completely crumbled in that moment. The Reed she'd known eight years ago hadn't even really liked kids. He'd certainly never had the time of day for them—more focused on his own needs and wants. It had been the same way with them as well—she'd always felt he chose himself over her, which was exactly what she'd been afraid had happened when she thought he'd left her at the altar for a movie role.

But this Reed? He was his niece's date to a Daddy/Daughter Dance and letting her paint his fingernails.

Teagan wasn't sure her ovaries could handle it.

She cleared her throat. "Well, let's get started. I'll put on some music and we'll learn a few moves, okay?"

"Okay!" Nell shouted, already getting more comfortable and grabbing the bar, swinging her body below it. "I'm a good dancer. Addison is just a meanie. I always get the high score on my Wii."

Teagan chuckled, loving that the young girl's only frame of reference for dancing was an interactive video game. "Well, that just sounds amazing."

She turned on some music and then instructed Reed and Nell to stand together and walked them through a few different simple dances that would be sure to impress her classmates. An hour later, Nell was more confident than ever and was practically bouncing around the studio, asking if they could go to the dance immediately.

"It's not till this weekend, Nell," Reed reminded her, calling across the studio. He turned to Teagan and lowered his voice. "When I get out of here tonight, can I come find you?"

Teagan's tongue slid across her lower lip. "I'm going home early tonight."

"I'll come there then." Reed stepped even closer, his hand tracing a line up her arm. "I need to be with you, Teag. Do you want that? Do you want me?"

"Yes." Her voice was breathy and soft, completely unexpected. "Come tonight."

He grinned mischievously. "I plan to. After you." Leaning in, he placed a soft kiss against her cheek. "See you tonight, beautiful." He pulled away and turned to find his niece. "Come on, Nell. Let's go find your mom before she gets kicked off set for stalking every celebrity she can find."

Nell laughed and hugged her arms around her own torso. "Mom said she's going to find McDreamy. She said he's her hall pass, but Mom isn't in school. Why does she need a hall pass?"

"I, uh, well you see...okay, that's..." Reed put out his glittery pink hand and she interlaced her little fingers with his. "Let's just go. Mom can explain it to you."

Teagan watched them go, trying to suppress her laughter. She was beginning to realize that there was no questioning them anymore. She was in love with Reed Scott. She always had been, and despite years apart and a hatred that could kill, she'd never stopped loving him. She'd never stopped wanting him.

Now he was back, and he wanted to be hers. She just had to decide if she wanted to be his.

CHAPTER SIXTEEN

"BENSON, you need to be on your best behavior." Teagan wagged a finger at her cat where he sat sprawled on the ottoman in front of her couch.

She finished folding a throw blanket and draped it on the back of her couch. Though her apartment hadn't been very untidy, she'd still spent the last thirty minutes cleaning up and making sure everything looked okay. This would be the first time Reed would see where she lived, and as much as she loved her tiny home, it was exactly that—tiny. Not to mention, it wasn't in the greatest area either.

But, she could afford it and it had a big window that got a ton of sun during the day which Benson loved. All in all, it was a great place and she was proud that she not only lived alone, but was able to do so in such an expensive area like Los Angeles.

Admittedly, she was considering moving once her lease was up now that she had a new check coming from her role in the movie. Doing double the work was exhausting, but signing that contract and looking at all those zeros? Worth. It.

A knock came from the front door, and Teagan whirled

around to look at it. "He's here, B." She checked herself in the mirror quickly, fluffing out her wavy brown hair and straightening the slouchy grey sweater she was wearing over a tight pair of dark jeans.

Finally, she opened the front door.

Reed was leaning against the door jam, a black leather jacket covering his broad shoulders and sculpted chest over a black pair of jeans. He lifted his gaze to hers, smoldering green eyes against his smooth olive skin, a slightly scruffy beard shaping his jaw. "Hey."

"Hi." She stepped aside to let him come in.

Reed stalked toward her and wrapped one arm around her waist, pulling her into his body. He knocked the door closed behind him and pressed his lips to hers.

She moaned and arched her body into his, already ready for him in every way. Circling her arms around his neck, she hopped up into his arms, anchoring her legs around his waist.

He lifted her, his hands on her ass. "Bedroom?" he whispered between kisses.

"Over there." She pointed to the other side of a bookcase where her bed was hidden in the small studio apartment.

He kicked off his shoes as she helped him shrug out of his jacket as he walked them over to the bed. They tumbled on to the bed together, pulling clothes off in every direction as she suddenly felt a frenzy in her body that only he could satisfy.

"I need to taste you," Reed whispered in her ear, gripping the top of her jeans and pulling them down her legs, then tossing them off.

"Yes, please," she breathed, already panting and writhing beneath him.

He pushed her knees apart, kissing down her naked body, taking care to pause at her nipples and roll his tongue around each one. Sliding his tongue over her stomach, he made his way down to the apex between her legs and spread her knees farther apart.

Instead of where she'd expected him, she felt Reed pressing his lips against her leg. Glancing down, she saw him kissing a line down her scar. She swallowed hard, loving the gesture and struggling to not feel tainted because of the ugly mark on her body.

The way he kissed her, the way he cherished every inch of her—even the parts she cringed at—made her feel whole and beautiful and accepted exactly the way she was.

His lips moved to her inner thigh and then up. The moment his tongue touched her center, she nearly exploded off the bed. "Reed!"

"Mmm," he moaned against her, flicking his tongue across her clit before diving farther inside her. His hands gripped the outside of her thighs, holding her quivering legs still as he kissed, licked, and nipped her most sensitive spots as she pumped her hips against him.

Moving one arm in, he slid his finger across her and pressed it inside. His tongue continued to lap at her clit as two fingers thrust in and out of her. It didn't take long for the perfect combination to have her hurdling toward her climax.

"Oh, God, Reed...I'm going to come." She couldn't stop the waves of pleasure that were already beginning to pummel her body.

"Good." He growled and nipped at her. "Come for me. Now."

She shattered immediately, trembling as he sped up and took everything she was offering him. "Ahh..." Stars splintered behind her eyelids as her body jolted and spasmed and she had to concentrate just to catch her breath.

Reed leaned over the side of the bed and grabbed a foil packet from the pocket of his jeans on her bedroom floor. Rolling on the condom, he climbed over her and hiked up her knees to be against his side. He pressed against her core, playing with her entrance as he circled around. "Teag..."

"Mmm?" She gripped his shoulders and pushed her hips against his, wanting him inside her.

"Are you sure about this?" he asked.

She opened her eyes, staring into his. It was a simple question, but there was so much packed inside. He wanted her to be all in with him. He was all in. Doing this...was all in. Literally.

That was exactly what she wanted.

Nodding her head, she leaned forward and kissed him. "Fuck me, Reed."

He grinned, and in one long motion, he slammed inside her to the hilt. The way he filled her made her feel delirious in how intoxicating it was, and yet, at the same time, incredibly filling and almost painful. His size had always been impressive, and she'd forgotten how much so until right now.

As he pulled back out, then thrust forward again, she stretched and adjusted around him. Every new movement felt even better than the last, and they fell into a rhythm where their bodies worked in blissful harmony. "God, Teag...you feel amazing," he whispered against her ear, nibbling on her ear lobe. "I can't get enough of you."

"Mmm," she moaned against neck, writhing beneath him and thrusting her hips in motion with his. "It's as perfect as I remember."

He slightly gripped her hair and pulled back, exposing even more of her neck to him. His tongue slid across her throat and then down to her breasts, taking her nipple into his mouth and swirling his tongue around the tip. "I remember everything about you."

His breath tickled against her skin, and she shivered. "Everything?"

He nodded, slamming into her again and then reaching

between them. "Like you much you love this." His fingers circled her clit, rubbing hard as he continued to thrust inside her.

Teagan's back arched, and she moaned deeper, shocked that she was already so close to coming again. "Oh, God..."

"Come on me, Teag," he instructed, going harder and faster as her body began to break open once more. She shattered against him, groaning into his shoulder as she bit down and left a mark. He held her as tightly to his body as possible, pumping in to her several more times until she felt him begin to shake, emptying inside her. "Fuck. That was...that was amazing."

Teagan could barely find her breath, gasping and panting beneath him as he slowly rolled off her to the side. "It was everything." And literally, that was all she could think.

It was every bit as amazing as she'd remembered from when they'd had sex years ago, and yet, it was so much better. It wasn't young and frenzied anymore, but rather mature and knowing. He knew how to manipulate her body exactly how she needed it, and there was no doubt in her mind that he'd felt everything she had. The heaviness of the emotion and intimacy between them, the intense dynamic of knowing that nothing about this was just physical. Nothing about this was just sex.

He brushed a piece of hair off her face, propping himself up on his elbow as he lay on his side and stared at her. "Teag?"

She turned to face him, curling into his perfect chest and ridiculously sculpted abs. She draped her arm over his waist, and sighed. "Yeah?"

Reed tipped her chin so she was looking up at him. "I love you. I'm *in* love with you. I never stopped."

She searched his eyes for a moment, caught off guard by his sudden admission. "Reed..."

"I'm not asking for you to say it back. I just wanted you to know," he continued. "Because, I can't not say it. I can't look at you, touch you, kiss you, and not have you know that I love you with every fiber of my being. That I'll spend the rest of my life proving that to you, and proving that this time—if you want it—it's forever."

A lump formed in her throat, and she closed her eyes for a moment, willing the tears away. "I want to say...that. I just...it scares the hell out of me."

He leaned in and kissed her. "Anything worth having is worth fighting for. I'm going to fight for you, Teag."

She tightened her grip around his waist, pulling herself in closer to him, skin to skin. "I want that."

"*Meow!*" Benson jumped on the bed beside them and climbed directly on top of Reed's shoulder.

"Good God!" Reed jolted, surprised. He pushed Benson off of him. "That thing is still alive?"

"Benson is immortal," she said, laughing. "And he was always one of your biggest fans."

"The feeling is not mutual," Reed teased, but he was already giving Benson little scratches behind his ears. Benson purred and rubbed against them. "This is weird while I'm naked."

Teagan shrugged. "Cats don't believe in boundaries."

CHAPTER SEVENTEEN

"GOOD LUCK, TEAGAN!" One of the production assistants waved at her from across the parking lot as she walked toward the set.

She waved back excitedly. "Thanks!"

Today was the last day she'd be filming on *Break Down*, though there were still a few more days during which her other cast mates would be finishing up their scenes. It had been a whirlwind three months, and Teagan still couldn't believe everything that had happened.

Three months ago, she'd been part of the crew and harboring a nearly decade-long hatred for her ex-fiancé who'd left her at the altar. Now, she was dating and falling back in love with him and had a pivotal role on the cast. Talk about life throwing curveballs.

She arrived on set a minute later and spotted Reed already talking to the director and preparing for his scene. He winked at her and she felt that familiar warmth swirling in her gut at the mere thought of him.

"Teagan Reynolds?" A voice called out behind her.

She turned around to see a tall, bald man in a business suit sporting an incredibly expensive watch. "Yes?"

He stuck out his hand toward her. "My name is Jason Allen. I'm an agent, and I think we should talk."

"Oh, right." She remembered the name. "You're with Reed, right?"

"Reed Scott? I am, but I also sign new talent," he said. "I'd like to discuss that with you."

She furrowed her brow. Getting an agent hadn't even crossed her mind at this point. "You want to sign me?"

"Without a doubt. I actually have an open role lined up, and the moment I heard about it, your name popped into my mind." He looked so sure of himself, but she had no doubt that his salesman pitch was well rehearsed. "Let's go grab a seat in your dressing room, and I can go over the paperwork with you."

She debated declining him, but, honestly, she was eager to hear what he had to offer. After this current role was over, she had nothing else lined up. She'd stumbled into this job by dumb luck—or bad luck, in Taylor's case—and it was doubtful that was going to happen again. If she wanted to keep up the pace and stay in front of the camera, she needed to be planning her next move in Hollywood.

"I have a few minutes before filming if you don't mind hair and makeup being there," she agreed, then motioned in the direction of her dressing room. She could talk while they prepped her for filming, but other than that, she didn't have a free moment to spare.

"Works perfectly for me," he replied, following her.

Her hairdresser and makeup artist were already set up in her room and waiting for her. Steele, her makeup artist, was borrowed from her sister, Aria. They were best friends, and Steele was every bit as full of personality as she was full of talent. Vibrant silver hair, colorful makeup, and her ears cuffed by dozens of earrings, she was an eclectic beauty. Teagan just felt lucky that she could utilize her talents for this role.

The team quickly ushered her into the chair and got to work. Jason leaned against the vanity counter and handed her a manila folder full of paperwork.

Teagan opened it and scanned over the contract he'd handed her. "Is this...is this for Broadway? *Cats: The Revival?*" Teagan's eyes widened, and she lifted her gaze to his. "Are you being serious right now? I heard this was going to be huge."

"The Big Apple, darling," Jason confirmed. "There's an open spot for the cat, Jennyanydots. You'd be perfect for it. It's not super heavy on the singing, but it is heavy on dancing. You'd be onstage on one of the biggest shows Broadway's ever seen."

"This is incredible." *Cats* had been one of her favorite shows of all time, and she'd put seeing the revival on her bucket list. But to actually be in it? That hadn't even crossed her mind. "When are auditions?"

"No audition necessary, if you sign with me." Jason crossed his arms over his chest. "I have exclusive access to this spot, and I already convinced them of how perfect you are. Showed them some B-roll from this movie, and they're sold."

Teagan blinked hard, trying to process the news. "Wow. Well, I mean, I have to think about it. I have to talk to my mother...she's my manager. Or she was when I was doing this professionally."

She didn't want to admit that there was a lot more to think about than just what her family would think. Moving across country? That was a huge step, one she certainly hadn't planned for.

"Of course, talk to anyone you want. Just keep in mind that if we want this, we have to move fast."

She nodded. "I understand."

"Good." With that, he pulled out another envelope from his suit pocket. He waited a moment until the makeup artist had finished applying her mascara, and then handed it to her. "Here's the contract for my agency. If you're interested, give it a sign and I'll come pick it up."

Teagan took the envelope from him, and then paused. "Jason, can I ask a question?"

"Always. Anything for a client." He grinned and leaned back against the vanity.

Inhaling a deep breath, she decided to just go for transparency. "Are you...are you offering me a job across the country to separate Reed and me? Is this about him?"

Jason's eyes tinged darker, and the smile slipped from his lips. "Well, I'm not going to lie. Reed is a client of mine and keeping him clean and out of the public spotlight for a while is pretty important to his career."

"Dating me isn't...clean?" That just sounded rude. She wasn't some party girl or skanky sorority slut that would make him seem like a playboy. Hell, they'd known each other over a decade. "Excuse me?"

"It's not about you," he assured her. "It's about your history."

"I don't have any skeletons in my closet," she replied, definitely offended now. This was some bullshit, and she could feel the steam rising inside her. "If anything, Reed is the one with the skeletons—not me."

She wasn't trying to throw him under the bus or anything, but she knew his agent already would know the details if he was any good at his job. Plus, she didn't like feeling she was the problem here. If anything, she was a goddamn saint for forgiving the notorious Reed Scott. A little credit would be nice, instead of being called *dirty*.

Honestly—what the fuck.

Jason tilted his head to the side. "This isn't just the best move for you, Ms. Reynolds. It's also the best move for him, and he knows it."

"He knows about this?" Teagan held up the contract. "He

thinks I'm going to taint his reputation?" Fury swirled inside her now at both this damn agent and Reed. The man she was falling in love with again, the man who was doing everything to win her back...wanted her to leave? She didn't buy it. There was no way. "*He* is the one who left *me* at the altar. *He* is the one who abandoned *me* when I nearly died. Those are *his* skeletons —not mine."

She was shocked those admissions even came out, but, damn, this man put her on edge.

Jason's eyes flitted to Steele and the hairdresser briefly, then back to Teagan. "That's exactly my point. I'd rather keep those stories quiet, but if you two are seen together, reporters are going to go digging in to your past—into *his* past."

She contemplated what he was saying, but it was all way more than she could process right now. There was no way Reed knew about this or would agree to it. He wouldn't want to send her across the country, and he definitely wouldn't think she would be a black mark on his career.

Right?

Even though she was calling bullshit, this was still an amazing offer and one she couldn't just turn down without at least considering it. "I'll look it over."

"That's all I ask." With that, he gave her a quick nod of his head and then headed out of the dressing room.

"What an asshole," her hairdresser said as soon as the door was closed.

Teagan laughed. "He was a dick, but isn't most of Hollywood?"

"You've got a point there, girl." Steele chimed in next. "Hollywood will eat you alive if you let it."

Her hair dresser finished styling Teagan's high pony. "Are you going to take the role? I mean...asshole or not, money is a language all of us speak."

Teagan gave a short chuckle, but the truth was she didn't know. The offer was incredibly tempting. But she and Reed had only just started their second chance at romance a little over two months ago. Everything had been going wonderfully, and even her family was finally on board—which had taken *major* convincing.

But she'd gone down this road before. She'd received a role on Broadway and turned it down—for Reed. Now, an agent wanted her to take a role on Broadway—for Reed. Somehow, it was still all for him.

Whether it was the role or the man she loved, she was going to lose something she wanted. And Reed was in the middle of everything. *Déjà vu.*

"I honestly don't know," she admitted. "I guess we'll see."

CHAPTER EIGHTEEN

"WELL, YOU HAVE TO TAKE IT." Aria looked over the top of her martini glass from the other side of the restaurant table. "I mean, you can't turn down a role in *Cats*. This revival is supposed to be huge. Like, *huge*."

Simone nodded her head. "Seriously, Teag. Actors make bicoastal relationships work all the time. This doesn't have to be a deal breaker, but turning it down? That would be the deal breaker for me."

Aria sighed. "You already left a role for him, remember?"

"I remember," Teagan assured them.

"And then he stood you up at the—" Aria continued.

"Oh, good Lord. If I hear one more mention of that stupid wedding, or any of that shit, I'm going to lose my mind." Teagan took a long swig out of her glass of wine. "I forgave him. You guys need to, too."

As much as she loved grabbing lunch with her sisters, there were always plenty of squabbles between them. None of it mattered in the long run, because this was her family. These women were her ride-or-dies, and she'd do anything for them.

Simone shrugged. "I don't think it's that we haven't forgiven him. It's that you haven't told him the full story."

"Exactly," Aria chimed in. "Which is sketchy and makes us feel like there must be a reason for that. Why haven't you told him your car accident was right after the wedding?"

"There's no good way to tell someone that," she replied, waving the waiter over for another glass. "It would just hurt him. Some stories aren't meant to be told."

"Oh, he's going to be fucking devastated," Simone said. "But better he finds out from you than someone else. You said even his agent knows."

She did have a point on that one, though she couldn't imagine that being a topic that would just randomly come up. Especially with how seriously his agent was trying to protect him from that story.

"Well...how do I even tell him?" she asked, swirling the wine in her fresh glass of wine. "How do you basically tell someone you almost died and, in a tangential way, it's his fault."

"You start with not sugarcoating it. It was *definitely* his fault," Aria reminded her. "You had just left your almost-wedding. You wouldn't have been in that car, crying your eyes out, if it wasn't for him standing you up at the altar minutes before."

"But, she has a point. That doesn't make it *entirely* his fault," Simone defended her.

Aria shook her head. "I promise you, he's not going to see it that way. If he's a good guy and he truly loves you, then he's going to blame himself. It's how he handles that guilt that's going to tell you what kind of man he is."

"What do you mean?" Teagan asked. "No one would handle news like that well."

"Yeah, but will he make it about you? Will he apologize and do anything he can to make it up to you? Or will he make it about himself, beat himself up and focus only on how shitty he feels."

Aria had another point. Sometimes she hated how bossy her older sister was, but the truth was, she knew what she was talking about. And even more than that, she had Teagan's best interest at heart first and foremost. There's nothing more important in sisterhood.

Teagan took in a deep breath and thought about the fact that she'd be seeing Reed for dinner later tonight. "I'll...I'll try. I'll try to tell him tonight."

"Only if you're ready," Simone urged. "You can't just throw it out there like a grenade."

"Facts," Aria agreed.

Easier said than done. She'd been carrying this live grenade and it could explode at any moment. Purposefully detonating it was going to hurt, but the question was would it hurt him? Or her?

Aria's phone rang, and she glanced down at the screen. "It's Ben. Give me a second, it could be about Tillie."

"Answer it," Teagan encouraged her.

"Hey, handsome," she practically sang into the phone. It was almost a little disgusting how much these two loved each other after five years together. Seriously, it was like they never left the honeymoon phase. Though, if Teagan was being honest, it was mostly jealousy on her part that made her feel that way.

Aria's eyes widened slightly, and then she gasped. "No!"

Simone and Teagan traded nervous glances.

"Yeah, squash it as fast as you can." She tapped her finger against the table irritably. "I don't care the cost. Kill the story." Aria nibbled on the edge of her lip.

The last time Aria had been at the center of a news story, it had been because of the nude photos of her and her director leaking to the press. Teagan couldn't stand to see her sister go through something so awful again.

"I'll tell her. I love you." Aria hung up the phone and placed it down on the table.

"Uh, share. Like now," Simone blurted out. "That sounded full of drama."

Aria took a deep breath, and then swung her gaze over to Teagan.

Shit. She sat up straighter. "It's about me?"

"There are pictures of you and Reed in *Hills Secrets Magazine*," Aria confirmed, citing one of the trashiest tabloids around Hollywood. Their paparazzi were known for being sketchy as hell and doing anything to get a damning photo.

"What kind of picture?" *Please, Lord, no.*

"Not like mine." Aria waved her hand between them. "Fully clothed, obviously. But...it's paired with an exposé."

Teagan swallowed. "About us?"

Aria slowly nodded. "About everything we were literally just talking about."

Teagan's stomach sank.

"Fuck." Simone groaned.

"I mean, it's only one part of the story," Aria explained. "They also talk about you guys falling in love and how everyone thinks you're perfect together. Apparently, some people on set talked to them and admitted that they've seen you all...I don't know, canoodling or whatever."

"How did they find out about the rest? About our history?"

"Ben said his sources say it was a hairdresser who leaked the story, brought it to their attention in the first place."

Fucking damn it all to motherfucking hell. She'd forgotten—even if only for a second—this was Hollywood, and people could be trusted only until someone else offered more cash. Her hairdresser had basically even said that.

"If it makes you feel better, Ben said you come off looking

great in the story." Aria fiddled with the stem of her wine glass. "I mean, all you did was fall in love."

Teagan swallowed the last of her wine, then pushed up from her seat, already opening the Lyft rideshare app on her phone. "I need to talk to Reed before he sees this."

"Good idea," Simone agreed. "Then find that hairdresser and beat the ever-loving shit out of her."

Tempting.

"We've got the tab," Aria assured her. "Go."

"Thanks, girls." Teagan slid her purse strap over her shoulder. "I love you both."

"Love you more," Simone replied. "Now get the hell out of here and find your man. Maybe he hasn't seen it yet."

She doubted that was possible, not with Jason Allen on his side, fighting his fires. There was no way his agent wouldn't be on top of that immediately. But...there was a chance.

Maybe she could salvage this. Or maybe she'd just destroyed everything she'd spent the last two months rebuilding.

CHAPTER NINETEEN

"Reed, open this goddamn door right the fuck now." Jason was standing outside his penthouse door, but Reed had absolutely zero plans on letting him inside. Sitting in a leather armchair in his office, he was sipping his third glass of scotch. "I know you're here, Reed. Open the fucking door because we need to talk."

He already knew what Jason wanted to talk about, and there was no damn way he could even fathom that conversation. Hell, he couldn't even fathom what he'd just learned. Talking about public relations and how to spin the story—that was just going to have to be Jason's job without him.

A second later, his phone rang and Jason's face popped onto the screen. Reed hit the dismiss option and downed the rest of the scotch in his glass. *Persistent fucker.*

Reed scrolled back through his text messages, looking at the half a dozen he'd received from Teagan today trying to reach him. She'd left voicemails too, but he couldn't listen to them. He couldn't talk to her after everything he'd just learned he'd done to her. Hell, he didn't even know how to look at her. Guilt swarmed his stomach, and he wanted to disappear, wishing he'd never forced his way back into Teagan's life in the first place.

God, she deserved so much better than him. All this time, she'd known what he'd done to her, and yet, she'd forgiven him and been willing to look past it all. He couldn't let her do that.

His phone rang again, and this time, he saw his friend Alistair's name.

"Hey, man," Reed answered the call.

"Down for a drink tonight, man?" Alistair asked, clearly already at the bar based on the loud music in the background. "The whole gang is down at Siegfried's. It's been forever since we've partied with your ass!"

Reed glanced at the copy of *Hills Secrets Magazine* in his left hand. The cover story staring back at him—Teagan, him, their entire life written in black and white for the world to see. Sure, not everything in it was true, but enough was to tell him their sources were credible.

"I'm already a few glasses in, but yeah. I'm coming. See you in twenty." He threw the magazine down on the hall table and pulled up the Lyft rideshare app on his phone. Ordering a car, he instructed it to meet him around back.

Within a few minutes, his ride had arrived, and Reed headed straight down to the back alley, bypassing Jason altogether. Minutes later, he was in the back seat of a black Range Rover, headed downtown.

Another call came through, and he glanced down at his phone. Teagan's smile lit up his screen, and the familiar guilt rolled in his stomach. He briefly considered declining the call, but after everything he'd already done to her, he couldn't do that, too.

"Hey," he answered.

"Hey, Reed. I've been trying to reach you all day. I have something I need to talk to you about." Teagan's voice was melodic as usual, but there was a hesitance to it that he hadn't heard before. Though he was beginning to wonder if it had always been there, and he just hadn't been paying attention.

There was so much he'd missed, so many signs he'd ignored—and for what? To pursue his own happiness at her expense? All this time, he hadn't known how badly he'd been hurting her—had hurt her in the past—and she'd said nothing. She'd just forgiven him and protected his feelings.

Fuck, she deserved so much better.

"Are we still on for dinner tonight?" she asked.

Reed shook his head, even though she couldn't see him. "Something came up. I'll have to reschedule."

"Um, okay," she responded slowly. "It's kind of urgent, though. I was hoping we could talk."

"Later. I'm sorry." With that, he hung up the phone.

Tears stung at his eyes as he stared out the window at the streets of Los Angeles speeding by, but he refused to let them spill over. He felt like such an asshole for ending their conversation like that, but he couldn't bear to hear what she had to say. He couldn't hear her tell him how he'd almost killed her, how it was his fault that her career and life had come to a screeching halt.

He couldn't hear her confirm what he'd read in that fucking tabloid.

All he'd done was stop by the grocery store to grab a bottle of wine on his way home from the set. Just a simple bottle of wine to pour over dinner with Teagan. He'd already picked up steaks and potatoes and was planning on cooking her a nice meal to enjoy in front of his fireplace.

Checking out, he'd ignored the tabloids lined up in each check out aisle. Nine times out of ten, he didn't even glance at them. He was so used to seeing his face splashed across the covers that it didn't even faze him anymore—but it wasn't his face that gave him pause. It was Teagan's. Her arms wrapped around his neck as she leaned up and kissed him on a back lot where they had been sure no one could see them.

Clearly, someone had.

Against his better judgment, he'd picked it up and turned to the coordinating article inside. An even larger picture of Teagan laughing and holding his hand stared back at him. He looked so happy in the photo, serene almost—an entirely different side of him than he'd ever seen on display before. For a minute, he'd almost been pleased with the spread. He wanted the world to know the beautiful brunette on his arm was his.

But then he'd read the article.

He'd read how the reporter had uncovered their past—college sweethearts turned sour at the wedding chapel. They put together the timeline of the movie he'd first starred in, stating that was why he'd left her. A lie, for sure, but he couldn't fault them that the timing was shitty at best.

The invasion of privacy was irritating, but it was the next part of the article that sent him reeling. Sources revealed that Teagan's career-ending injury occurred on her drive home from the chapel. She'd been so distraught, she hadn't seen the oncoming car until it was too late. There was a photo of her in a hospital bed, and she looked more dead than alive. How they even got the photo, he didn't know—but there was no mistaking the dates in the corner.

Their wedding date.

At first, he'd thought it was another lie. A fabricated scandal to sell more copies. But when Jason started blowing up his phone, Reed realized there must be truth to it. Jason wouldn't bother him over tabloid theatrics unless it were real.

This was real.

He'd made the worst decision of his life, and she'd almost lost hers in the process.

Reed's jaw tensed, shallow breaths forcing in and out. He

wasn't sure he could handle this. He wasn't sure he could ever forgive himself for what he'd done to her. There was certainly no way in hell she'd forgive him.

So why had she started dating him again?

He swallowed hard when they turned into the parking lot of the bar his friend was at. The only answer seemed to be that she was as angelic as the article described her to be, as wonderful as he had always known her to be. She'd forgiven him for almost taking her life, for leaving her at the altar, for everything he'd ever done to her.

And that was the problem. He didn't deserve that.

He didn't deserve her.

Reed thanked the driver and climbed out of the car. The moment he turned around, flash bulbs went off in his face. He squinted his eyes, trying to see past the dots and haziness now fogging his vision as more cameras clicked.

A reporter got right up in his face. "Reed Scott! Is it true you killed your ex-fiancée?"

"Did you leave the love of your life at the altar?" Another reporter shouted.

"Scott, are you a runaway groom?"

"Why didn't you visit your ex-fiancée at the hospital after she was injured on your wedding day?"

Reed gritted his teeth and stared down the asshole who'd asked the last question. "Get the hell out of my way."

The throng of reporters only pushed closer, and Reed began to back up, trying to figure how to get away from the crowd.

"Tell us, Reed—why did you abandon the woman you claimed to love on your wedding day?" the same reporter asked again.

Reed tried to slip around him, but he blocked his way.

"Did you destroy her career?"

He gritted his teeth, ducking his face from the camera lens

and trying once again to push through the crowd of shouting paparazzi. Reed was trapped between the brick wall of the bar and the crowd of cameras when he heard the reporter call out one more time.

"Is it your fault she almost died? Did you even care?"

Reed stopped in his tracks, and before he could even register what was happening, he was on top of the reporter. Whether it was the booze already in his system or the fury at the reporter's accusation, he'd reaching his boiling point. He slammed the camera into the concrete, shattering it, and then his fists were flying. Reed pummeled the reporter repeatedly while the crowd desperately tried to pull him off.

Someone finally managed to yank him off, but the police were already running up to the crowd.

"He tried to fucking kill me!" the reporter on the ground yelled. "Arrest him!"

The police officer turned to a panting Reed and pulled out his cuffs. "Turn around, sir."

Reed said nothing. Being arrested wasn't anything new, given his previous reputation. He turned around and put his hands behind him as the officer grabbed him roughly and locked his wrists together.

The entire time he was being read his rights, all he could think about was one thing—Teagan was better off without him, and now the whole world knew that.

CHAPTER TWENTY

"I'M LITERALLY GOING to kill him," Aria said, pouring them both another glass of wine.

Teagan sniffed, wiping her face of tears for the umpteenth time today. "It could just be a misunderstanding."

"Hard to misunderstand 'arrested for public intoxication and assault and battery,' babe." Aria squeezed Teagan's hand. "He stood you up to...what? Get drunk with his friends and beat up a photographer?" She shook her head, sighing. "You deserve better than him, Teag."

She swallowed, not wanting to hear that at all. She wanted to believe Reed had changed. She wanted to believe that the universe had brought them back together for a reason, and that he was every bit the man she'd remembered...and hoped he'd be again.

She didn't want to know that nothing had changed. That he was every bit the partier the tabloids accused him of being. That he still bailed on her when the going got tough.

"I told you yesterday—how he'd respond to this news would be how you'd know if he deserved you or not. Did he come and apologize, beg for your forgiveness, act like a damn man?" Aria took a few swallows from her glass of wine. "Nope. He just went off and got all hotheaded like some sort of caveman."

Teagan didn't say anything, because there really was no defense she could offer. She wanted more than anything to be able to explain away what he'd done, but the only explanation was dismal at best.

She hadn't even gotten the chance to talk to him herself, though there was no doubt in her mind at this point that he'd seen the article. Hell, his agent had already been trying to get her to sign a non-disclosure so she wouldn't speak to the press about their history.

Not that she ever would. Their story was theirs, and she had zero plans on letting anyone else into it.

Or maybe there was no story anymore. Honestly, she wasn't sure. It certainly felt like they were over...like he'd closed the chapter on them and walked away. He might not have said it in so many words, but his silence was deafening, and she'd heard it all before.

Benson jumped up into her lap, and she absentmindedly patted him. "I need to talk to Reed," she told her sister. "I need to understand what happened. Tabloids lie, and we don't really know the truth."

Aria shrugged. "I mean, I agree. You two should talk, but I think the story is pretty clear cut here."

A knock came on her apartment door, and she instinctively hoped it was Reed.

Aria glanced between her and the door. "Do you want me to get it? Do you think it's him?"

"I'll get it," she replied, putting the cat down and walking toward her front door. Taking a deep breath, she glanced through the peephole. "Ugh."

She swung the door open. "What do you want, Jason?"

"Lovely to see you, too, Ms. Reynolds." The agent waltzed through the doorway like he owned the place. "Nice studio you've got here. Fat cat."

Teagan picked up Benson defensively. "He's husky."

Jason didn't seem to care but pulled out a stack of papers from his briefcase and placed them on the counter. "We've got some paperwork to go over, Ms. Reynolds. Oh, hello, Mrs. Lawson." Jason finally seemed to notice Aria standing in the kitchen. "Good to see you, as always."

"Wish I could say the same," she replied, lifting one brow. Aria had never been a fan of agents in general, though Jason Allen rarely made friends if it wasn't for his benefit.

Teagan couldn't help but snicker at her comment. "What kind of paperwork?"

"The contract for your role in the Broadway show has been finalized, and it's ready for you to sign." He held up a pen toward her. "And, then there's the non-disclosure agreement we discussed."

"I already told you that I'm not signing that."

"The contract or the NDA?"

She nibbled on the edge of her lip. "The NDA, certainly. I'm not going to talk to the press about Reed. You don't have to worry about that."

"Ms. Reynolds, indulge me. He's my client, and he deserves every bit of protection as you do. That protection has already been violated by you once, and I have zero plans on allowing it to happen again."

"Me?" Teagan balked at the accusation. "I've not said anything to anyone."

"You spoke pretty freely in front of that hairdresser, putting us in this predicament to begin with," Jason reminded her.

"Only because *you* were basically accusing me of ruining

Reed's life." Teagan put her hands on her hips. "I'd not have been saying anything at all if you weren't there."

"Well, what's done is done," he replied. "But this contract? It's the best move for you here, Ms. Reynolds. This role is once in a lifetime, and to turn it down for a man currently behind bars certainly doesn't seem to be a desirable move."

"He's still in jail?" Her voice was smaller now. She'd been trying to figure out where Reed was, or why she hadn't heard from him for the past four days. Her calls had all gone unanswered, and she'd even tried going by his home to no avail. She'd assumed he'd been bailed out immediately, but apparently not.

Aria stepped closer, placing her hands on the counter. "Teag, this role is huge. You can't turn it down. Talking to Reed...it can wait. He's made his choice already, and it wasn't you."

Teagan swallowed hard, trying to wrap her head around the fact that her sister was actually agreeing with one of the most cunning and sleazy agents she'd ever met. They both did have a point...she couldn't—and wouldn't—turn down this role.

Plus, she didn't really owe him an explanation. He'd been the one who hadn't wanted to talk and had ignored most of her calls before he'd been arrested. He'd stood up their date to go get drunk. She wasn't going to wait around and hope he'd decide to talk to her when he got out of jail, when she really should just jump on this opportunity before it was too late.

If he wanted to talk when he got out of jail...he'd know where to find her.

"I'll sign the contract," Teagan agreed. "But only that. I'm not signing the non-disclosure agreement. I'm not going to talk to the press about us, but Reed...he doesn't deserve to control my silence."

Jason's jaw clenched, and he exhaled loudly. "Okay, fine. Let's do this." He handed her a pen. "Sign here."

She looked over the contracts quickly, and everything seemed the same as when her lawyer had reviewed it.

Teagan signed and then handed the pen back to him. "Done."

"Great. Your flight is booked for tomorrow, and you've got a studio apartment waiting for you a block from the theatre. I'd suggest getting your affairs in Los Angeles in order as quickly as possible. Rehearsals start in two days."

Teagan's eyes widened. "That's barely enough time to prepare."

She didn't want to sound ungrateful—hell, she was ecstatic. This role was everything she'd ever wanted in her career, and she'd never had any intention of turning it down.

"That's show business, baby," Jason said, tossing his arms up. "It doesn't stop for anyone."

Teagan looked toward her sister, but Aria just looked sad. She was frustrated that Reed was ruining this moment for her. Teagan wanted to feel ecstatic. She wanted to be jumping up and down with her sister, screaming with excitement at a lifelong dream fulfilled. She wanted to be celebrating a victory that at one point in her life had seemed absolutely impossible.

Instead, all she was thinking about was Reed, and her heart ached at everything she was losing.

CHAPTER TWENTY-ONE

"REED SCOTT," a corrections officer called out into the large cell where he was being held with half a dozen other men. "Bail's been made."

Reed stood from the rickety wooden bench and made his way out toward the front of the precinct where he saw his younger sister standing, nervously wringing her hands.

"Penelope?" Reed furrowed his brows. "What are you doing here?"

She put her hands on her hips. "Bailing you out, obviously."

"Where's Nell?" He looked around for his niece, but thankfully he didn't see her. There was no way in hell he'd want her to see him like this—behind bars in jail, still wearing rumpled clothing from five days ago. He shouldn't have even been in there so long for what he'd been charged with, but some old warrants had tripped him up for a while. To say he was irritated would be a freaking understatement.

"As if I'd bring my daughter to pick up her uncle in jail." Penelope rolled her eyes. "Come on. Let's get out of here. The car's out back."

He finished signing the paperwork the desk officer set before him, and the officer handed him back his personal effects in a bag, which was pretty much just his wallet and cell phone. He followed his sister out of the precinct through the back door to avoid any press. They hopped in the car quickly and drove off.

"We're going to my house, by the way. You're going to stay there." His sister aimed the car away from Los Angeles and in the direction of her home in the suburbs. "You're not going to be alone in a penthouse surrounded by photographers."

He didn't argue. Instead, he leaned against the window and watched the landscape fly by. She wasn't wrong, either. There was no way he'd want to try and get through a throng of photographers again. He was embarrassed he'd tried to do it at all—and failed spectacularly.

Reed pictured the bloodied face of the photographer he'd punched. Guilt washed over him, though he tried to shake it away. Luckily, he'd been informed that despite a few scratches and bruises, the reporter was fine. The things they'd said to him, the questions they'd asked—it was too much, too far. Whether or not that made his outburst excusable was another question he wasn't sure he wanted to answer right now.

He pictured the photo of Teagan lying in that hospital bed. She'd told him about her accident, and he'd seen the scars. He'd already hated the fact that he hadn't been there to help her through that. No matter what had happened between them, he should have been there. But to know it had happened after their non-wedding? When she was probably crying and not paying as much attention to the road as she should have been?

He was fucking devastated.

Reed swallowed hard, trying to keep the lump in his throat at bay. Was there anything he hadn't taken from her? He'd loved her with everything inside him for years, and then he'd not only left her standing at their wedding altar but then alone in a hospital bed. He'd taken her wedding, her future marriage, and then her entire career—all because he hadn't been mature enough to have an adult conversation with her before making such a rash decision.

Shame welled in him, and it was damn near unbearable.

"Are you going to call her?" Penelope glanced sideways at him as they drove.

Reed didn't respond. He didn't even nod his head. He had no idea. Part of him wanted to call and explain, beg her forgiveness and hope she hadn't even seen the news. Another part of him wanted to run and never see her again—for her sake. How much more pain could he cause her before he truly destroyed everything she was?

"Reed? The least you can do is talk to me. I did just pay your bail." His sister slapped his arm as they pulled off the freeway. "Don't be rude."

"Sorry." He sat up and ran his hands over his head. "I'm not trying to be rude. And I'm going to pay you back today, every cent."

"You fucking better," she said with a laugh. "Jackson'll kill you otherwise."

The corners of Reed's lips lifted into a small smile at the mention of his brother-in-law. He would definitely be furious when he found out Penelope had, once again, saved his ass. It wouldn't be the first time, and at this point, Reed wasn't even sure it would be the last time.

"I honestly don't know if I am going to call her," he admitted finally.

Penelope scoffed. "Then you're a bigger idiot than I thought."

He frowned. "Excuse me?"

"If that article is true, that girl has given up everything for you. Not just then, but now. She put aside all her fears, all of the past, all of the things you did to her, and she gave you another chance. She loved you—again. Or maybe she never stopped, I don't know." Penelope turned the car into her driveway and pulled up to the garage. "All I do know is that you owe it to her to talk to her. Apologize, and then either beg her forgiveness for the umpteenth time or let her go and give her the closure she probably needs."

Reed considered his sister's advice as he got out of the car. Despite the fact that she was his younger sister, he was always amazed at her wisdom and maturity. She definitely had him beat in that area.

His phone vibrated in the plastic bag in his pocket. He pulled it out then shoved the empty bag back down in his pocket. There were four missed calls from Jason, and a voicemail. Reed sighed and lifted the receiver to his ear. If he was lucky, his already low battery would die before he heard the whole message.

"Reed, I'm sending your sister to bail you out. You'll need to pay her back," Jason said in his voicemail. "I'd come myself, but I'm working on solving your issue. The reporter isn't going to press charges—I've talked to him. The tabloid is also not going to continue or follow up on the exposé. They can't do anything about it already being out there, but hopefully it'll just dissipate with the news cycle."

Reed sighed, hoping that was true. He wanted that story gone as much as his agent probably did.

Jason continued, "Oh, and one last thing, I got Reynolds a job in New York. She's already left, and I strongly suggest you leave her alone. Your reputation really can't handle another hit like this one, and you two are clearly fodder for entertainment news. But also—and I rarely get personal, so listen the fuck up—you've done enough to the poor girl. She's a spitfire, but she's clearly one of the better people in Hollywood, which is hard to find. Just...just leave her alone, Reed."

Reed clicked the delete button quickly and shoved the phone

back in his pocket. *Fuck.* He wanted to punch something, or cry; he wasn't sure which. That was probably the most humane he'd seen his agent be in a while. To see him defending Teagan and showing compassion, it meant something. He'd seen her while Reed was in jail, and if he was saying this, it meant she was hurting. It meant Reed had hurt her...again.

And then she'd left.

Part of him didn't even blame her. She should get as far away from his as possible. But then, in the same thought, he couldn't believe she hadn't even spoken to him. She hadn't even said goodbye. Had they ever really had anything if she could just cut him out of her life like that? Losing her like that—or at all—made him feel like his heart was being ripped out of his chest.

He knew he had no right to think or feel that, but he couldn't stop the frustration and hurt from building in him anyway.

Reed hoped Jason had gotten her a fucking amazing role, because anything less was unacceptable. She deserved this more than anything. This might be the big break she wanted, the one she had turned down to marry him.

He was not going to ruin it for her. Not again.

"Uncle Reed!" Nell came flying out the front door and threw herself against his legs. "You're here! Do you want to see my new doll?"

Reed laughed and hugged his niece, scooping her up into his arms as he walked her back into the house. "Sure, I'd love to."

"Good. I named her Teagan, after your friend!"

He swallowed and nodded, finally choking out, "That sounds great."

"Are we going dancing with her again?" Nell asked. "I want to go dancing again!"

"We'll see," Reed told her, unsure of how to really respond. Nell would forget about her question soon enough, but Reed wouldn't. He knew then and there that he couldn't just let her walk out of his life.

He wasn't going to ask her to come back to him, or for a second chance. Well, technically, a third chance. That ship had sailed, and he wouldn't let her put herself in harm's way again by being with him. But, she did deserve an apology. She deserved an explanation of some sort, and maybe a chance to yell at him. Hell, he'd let her punch him if she wanted. And for himself? He may not deserve it, but he needed a goodbye.

He needed to get his life in order first, but then he was going to go see her. He was going to give her the apology she deserved, and the closure that they both needed.

CHAPTER TWENTY-TWO

DID A TRUCK HIT ME?

It sure felt like one had...and then backed up and hit her again. Teagan's eyes blinked open slowly, and she took in her surroundings. Florescent lights. Tubes. Beeping monitors. A white board with a name on it followed by "R.N." next to a smiley face.

Why am I in a hospital?

"Teagan?" Her mother, Betty Reynolds, voice. She'd recognize that anywhere.

Slowly, she tried to turn her head to find where it was coming from, where her mother was, but her neck sent screeching pain roaring up and down her torso. Strangely, the pain stopped about mid-way down her spine. "Mom?"

"I'm here, baby. I'm here." Her mother's face came into view in front of her. "How are you feeling, Teagan?"

"Uh, not great..."

Her father, Jack Reynolds, chuckled, and she glanced over to where he stood at the foot of her bed. "That's an understatement, I'm sure."

"What happened?" Teagan asked, lifting her arm slowly to rub her head. Her limbs felt so heavy, so forced, and it was a struggle to do even that. As she rubbed her temple, a rush of memories came back to her.

Her white dress. Lace. She'd spent so many months looking for just the right one. The one he'd remember until they were old and gray.

Standing in that dress, her sister breaking the news that he was gone. She'd fallen to her knees, sobbing. Her chest pounded and ached, like he'd reached right in and pulled her heart from its safe haven behind her ribs.

Rushing from the chapel. She had to get out of there. She had to leave. He already had.

Tears falling against the steering wheel. She drifted just a little too far to the left. Just a few feet, barely anything. Except there was another car there, heading right for her.

Yanking the car to the right. She could fix this. She could save herself.

The smell of burned rubber. The screeching of twisted metal. Searing pain, and then nothingness. Black and cold, there was nothing.

Her dress was crumpled in a chair in the corner of the hospital room. It was streaked with black and red, rips and tears. Blood soaked through the lace, and it was almost beautiful if it hadn't been so painful.

"Mom?"

"Yes, baby." Her mother squeezed her hand.

"Am I going to be okay?"

Her mother tsked. "Why would you even ask that? Of course, you're going to be fine. You're alive, that's all that matters."

"Tell her the truth, Betty." Her father interrupted. "She needs to know. The doctors said she needs to know."

"Jack, no."

My father looked straight at me. "Teagan, move your toes."

She did.

He shook his head, and her mother looked away.

Frowning, Teagan pulled the blanket off her legs. Her first instinct was to cry, but she didn't. She just stared at the mangled mess of sutured and staples and metal braces holding her together. She wiggled her toes and she felt them moving, but her eyes...they saw nothing. Her toes didn't move. She felt it, but they didn't move.

"I... I'm paralyzed?" The words didn't even seem possible. She was a dancer. She'd just been offered a role on Broadway—one she'd turned down for him. But even so, it was how she moved, how she lived. Dancing was her identity. It's who she was. It was how she breathed.

No.

"No," she said out loud this time. "No. This isn't happening."

"Baby..." Her mother squeezed her hand again. "It's not the end of the world. It's going to be okay."

"It's the end of my world." Her voice was louder now. "And it's just not an option. It's not an option. This is not me. This is not my story."

Her mother looked at her with such sorrow and pain in her eyes. "Oh, Teagan. Of course not. You're so strong."

"You'll be okay, baby girl," her father said, rubbing her leg.

She watched him do it, but she didn't feel a thing.

This is not my story.

He *was not going to write her story.*

THE MEMORIES of that day flooded her as Teagan walked slowly across the stage of the famous Neil Simon Theatre, marveling at the fact that in just a few short days, she'd be performing there. The entire room seemed to be bathed in gold and was a stark contrast to the hospital room she'd laid in eight years ago.

She'd decided back then that her accident wasn't going to define her. She wasn't going to lose her dreams—and here she was. Sure, she'd gotten a little lost along the way, given up a few times, but, in the end, she was here. She was living the vision she'd set for herself in college.

It was insanely early in the morning, making her the only person on the stage aside from a janitor in the last row of the theatre vacuuming the aisles. The soft whir of his machine only added to the significance of the moment, vibrating through her like a crowd cheering and getting to their feet. She stared out at the rows and rows of chairs and the balconies above—almost fifteen hundred seats that would have almost fifteen hundred people every night watching her perform.

Well, not just her, but, damn, if it didn't feel like it.

Teagan dropped the cardigan from her shoulders, letting it hit the floor. She wiggled out of her sweatpants, leaving her in only a leotard and leggings, plus her dance shoes. These items were her second skin in many ways. She felt bare on stage, naked and vulnerable in a way that thrilled her and terrified her all at once. The tight fabric encased her, but it also stripped her of everything —her safety, her defenses, her excuses. She shed everything on stage when she danced, and it had led her to this moment.

Laid bare on this stage.

On her phone, she turned on the songs she'd be dancing to in the show and placed the phone on the stage. As it started, she moved with the melody. She pranced and paused and played with every lyrically beautiful, and yet, amusing, note to the famous songs.

She'd only been in New York City for a few hours, and yet the stage was the first place she'd come. Her suitcases were still sitting in the wings right next to Benson's cat carrier. He was fast asleep and didn't even seem to care about the cross-country trip he'd just been on. Her landlord was probably waiting for her, too, but she didn't care. This was a moment she'd waited for all her life, and now that she was here, she couldn't hold back.

Tears brimmed her lashes, but they were so different from the tears she'd been shedding lately. Those were heartbreak and disappointment...those were Reed's. But these? These tears were joy and freedom, and they were all hers.

Teagan leaped across the stage, coming to the big finish as the music reached a crescendo. When it did, and she landed back on her feet, she fell into a heap on the stage floor. She lay back and stared at the lights and walkways above her. Just stared.

It felt familiar, like it belonged and she belonged right there below it.

Like she was finally home.

Her cell phone interrupted her thoughts, ringing loudly through the empty theatre.

Teagan reached over and grabbed it, holding it to her ear. "Hello?"

"Did you get there safely?" Simone was on the other end.

Teagan smiled at her sister's concern. "I did. Simmy, it's beautiful."

"Oh, shit. You're never coming home."

She didn't reply right away, because honestly...she couldn't imagine leaving.

"Wait, did you seriously fall in love with New York that quickly?" Simone asked.

"It's magical, Simmy. The stage, the lights—the theatre is practically made of gold. Then outside, the streets, the people, the energy in the air..." Teagan sighed, dreamily continuing to stare up at the lights above her. "It's everything I am."

Simone chuckled. "Well, I'm glad you're happy. I'm going to miss you like crazy, though."

"Come visit soon!" Teagan offered. "From what I was told, my apartment is even smaller than the last one, so we'll have to spoon."

Simone laughed. "Cuddling is my specialty."

"I should probably go get my keys."

"You haven't moved in yet?" Simone asked. "Where are you?"

Teagan smiled, sitting up and looking out on the hundreds of empty seats in front of her. "I'm in the theatre. I just needed to see it."

"You always were a sentimental nut," Simone replied, chuckling again. "Well, I'll let you go lick the stage floor or whatever it is you're doing. Mom says to call her."

"Will do," Teagan replied. "Bye, love."

They cut the phone connection and Teagan stood and pulled on her sweatpants and cardigan, tucking the phone in her pocket. She walked to the very edge of the stage and looked down into the orchestra pit then back out onto the balconies. Inhaling slowly, she said a small prayer for her future performances—and for her future.

CHAPTER TWENTY-THREE

"I THINK that was our best performance yet," Betty, one of her co-stars, said as she carefully wiped away her stage makeup in the dressing room mirror. "Shit, this stuff is so hard to come off."

Teagan laughed, trying to wipe off her own stripes and whiskers that made her look like Jennyanydots, the cat. "This job is going to end up destroying my skin," she kidded, though it wasn't entirely far-fetched with the amount of makeup they wore daily. Eight shows a week would probably end up turning her into a zombie, but she didn't care one bit.

Spending the last month on Broadway had been one of the best experiences of her life, and it felt like everything was coming together just as it was falling apart. She hadn't spoken to Reed, but she'd seen from the papers that he was out of jail. It didn't really matter anyway, since she was across the country now, and she had zero plans to return anytime soon.

This was where she was meant to be, and for the first time in her life, she felt like she belonged. She'd loved Los Angeles, and she missed her family more than she could put into words, but something about the Big Apple spoke to her soul in a way that felt like home. Sure, she'd still visit from time to time, but she could already feel herself putting down anchors here in the big city.

Then there was her job. Being on stage every night, dancing and singing? It was her dream—eight years late, but it tasted just as sweet. Looking back on it now, she couldn't believe she'd once so willingly given this up for a man—even if that man had been the love of her life.

If it wasn't so embarrassing and pitiful, she'd laugh at her own stupidity. Especially since even with all she'd given up for him, he'd left anyway. It may have been a miscommunication, but he still left. *He left her.* Then, he'd swung back into her life with those green eyes and olive skin and perfect hair, and she'd opened her arms like it had never happened. She should have been more discerning, more unforgiving. She should have told him to get the hell away from her and never looked back.

She should have seen that a man who leaves once will leave again.

But despite her foolish forgiveness and their brief fling, she still came out on top. He was in the tabloids and fresh out of jail, and she was on Broadway living out her dreams. Nothing was going to make her lose this job, not if she had anything to say about it.

"Anything for Broadway," Betty sung theatrically, dancing over to the lockers and pulling out her regular street clothes. She began changing into them. "You work your whole life to get here, and then you lose the rest of your life to it."

"And there's nothing better," Teagan finished.

Betty nodded, smiling wide. She finished changing and began pulling her hair out of the pins it had been in under her wig. "You're damn right."

Teagan lifted her shirt over her head, finished wiping off her makeup, and headed to her own locker to grab her clothes.

"Ahem," a voice came from the doorway to the dressing room, then a small knock on the open door. "Teagan?"

She whirled around to see Reed standing there, averting his eyes from her half-unclothed body. "Reed? What are you doing here?"

"Can we talk?" he asked, not moving from the doorway.

Betty glanced between the two of them and then looked back at her. "Should I go? I can stay. Or go? I don't know what to do right now."

Teagan chewed on the edge other lips. "Could you give us a minute?" she finally asked.

Betty nodded and sidled up to her. "If you need anything, shout." Then she lowered her voice into a whisper. "He's hot!"

Teagan blushed, ignoring Betty as she slipped out the door past Reed.

Reed walked further into the room and closed the door behind him.

She went about finishing changing and unpinning her hair as well. "What are you doing here, Reed?"

"I thought we should talk."

She lifted one brow, pulling out the last of her pins in the mirror. "Did you? Interesting, because I would have thought so, too. A month ago."

"Teagan, can you pause for a minute?" He walked up behind her and placed his hands on her upper arms. "I want to talk."

She stared at his reflection in the mirror, letting down the last pin from her hair. Slowly, she turned around and faced him. There was barely any distance between them, and she became aware of her chest beginning to rise and fall, faster and faster. Deciding for a safer distance, she slipped around him and put a few feet between them.

"What do you want to talk about, Reed?"

He looked like he had so much to say, but he couldn't figure out where to start. "You left. You never even said goodbye, Teagan."

"You're mad?" She crossed her arms over her chest. "Did you seriously fly cross country to lecture me on goodbye etiquette?"

He paused, inhaling deeply. "No. I didn't. That doesn't mean we didn't deserve a goodbye. Is this it? Are we just over?"

"I got a job in New York, and you went to jail," she reminded him. If he thought he could come here and scold her, he was going to have another thing coming. "It's not exactly the foundation for a relationship, Reed."

"Fuck. I'm messing all this up. None of this is what I wanted to say." He pushed his hands into his pockets and looked up at her under his long lashes. "I'm sorry. That's what I came here to say. I'm so sorry, Teagan."

She swallowed, trying to figure out how to process those words coming from him. Something she wished she'd heard from him for years. "You're...you're sorry?"

He nodded. "I think it's overdue, don't you? That I apologize?"

"Depends." She crossed her arms over her chest. "What are you apologizing for?"

Reed inhaled slowly then blew it out in one long exhale. "Well, most recently, for standing you up. For going to jail. For disappearing on you last month. I was in such a bad place that night, and then when I got to the bar...I was just on edge. The paps were there, and I just exploded. There's no excuse for it."

She furrowed her brows. "You weren't already drunk and partying?"

"I'd already been drinking on my own," he admitted. "So, it's not much better."

Teagan appreciated his honesty, and he was right—it didn't make it better.

"But, more than that, I'm sorry for eight years ago. I'm sorry for leaving you at the altar, and for not being there when you were hurt.

That accident—it was my fault." Reed's voice cracked at the end. "I'm so fucking sorry that I let that happen, and you shouldn't forgive me. You should *never* forgive me for taking away so much from you." His face was twisted in so much pain and grief, that Teagan was caught off guard. "I promise you, I'll never forgive myself."

"Reed..." Teagan took a step toward him, placing her hand on his forearm. "I never blamed you for that accident. Not once."

He didn't look at her, but she could see the tears brimming his eyes. "You should."

"But I don't," she repeated. "I chose to get in that car. I chose not to take a moment to compose myself, or call a car, or have someone else drive me. Those were my decisions."

She stepped a little closer, this time taking his hand in hers. It was hard to stay angry or hurt when she could see how emotional he was about everything. He was being so vulnerable, so authentic...so raw. She couldn't add to his pain, and it was the truth. She never did blame him for her accident.

"The only things I hated you for was leaving me at the altar, and for not being there when I needed you." Teagan swallowed hard. "You didn't put me in that hospital bed, but you also never visited me. Not once."

"I didn't know. I swear, if I'd known..." Reed bit his bottom lip. "Nothing could have kept me away."

"You chose not to know, Reed. You disappeared. You didn't check in on me, or anyone. You left our friends and family behind, and you just...you started over." Teagan squeezed his hand. "You could have known."

He didn't say anything, but she could see him mulling it over in his mind. "You're right. I could have found out. I could have checked in."

"Why didn't you?" She wasn't sure she actually wanted to know the answer, but it had been eating away at her for years.

She couldn't fathom having been a part of someone's life every day for years, been in love, and then just...vanish. Start over with a new life. How could anyone do that to another person—or themselves?

She paused at the realization that maybe she'd just done the same thing. Had it been that easy to leave and chase her dreams? She wanted to believe that she'd have checked in on him, made sure he was okay...but she wasn't sure.

Reed ran his thumb across the back of her hand. "I thought I couldn't handle it. I thought if I spoke to you, or saw you, or even heard anything about you, I'd come running back."

Teagan's heart ached at the thought, and how familiar it felt. "Would that have been such a bad thing?"

"Looking back? Definitely not," he replied. "But at the time, I thought I was the road block standing between you and your future. I saw us both settling for a life in the suburbs with a white picket fence. With your talent, dreams...you deserve more than that."

Teagan let go of his hand, crossing her arms over her chest. "Bullshit."

"What?" He looked confused.

"That may be the reason you told yourself. Hell, it may even be true." Teagan wasn't about to let him fall on his martyrdom sword, not when she knew exactly what it felt like to chase her dreams over a relationship. "Did I have dreams? Sure. But would I have been happy with the white picket fence? If you were there, yes. I would have been the happiest woman alive. The rest would have figured itself out."

"Teagan..."

"No, let me finish," Teagan interrupted him, wagging her index finger. "You wouldn't have been happy with the white picket fence, and you saw settling down with me as losing your dreams. Don't play the martyr when there were just as many selfish reasons for what you did."

Reed looked startled and taken aback at her words. He didn't reply at first, leaning back against the makeup counter, as if to steady himself. Finally, he nodded his head slowly. "I think you might be right, but, fuck, that's hard to hear."

Teagan let her gaze drop, fiddling with a loose thread on her sweater.

"A part of me," Reed continued softly, "maybe a bigger part than I'd like to admit, saw marriage as the end game. We were so young, and our lives had barely started. There was so much I still wanted—fame, fortune, my acting career—and as shallow as that sounds, it was what was important to me back then."

She exhaled slowly, more relieved than she thought she would be to hear his admission.

"But, Teagan, I was an idiot. My priorities were incredibly off kilter, and that's what I admire you most for. You've never strayed from your values. You've always known who you are and what you wanted from life, and you went for it. But not once did you hurt other people to get it." Reed shook his head, a pain expression on his face again. "I wish I could say the same."

Teagan sighed, frustrated that he kept seeing her as some angelic being that she just wasn't. She was as flawed and human as he was. "I'm not some perfect princess, Reed. I left you to come here—remember?"

"It's not the same." Reed shook his head. "We were getting married, and I left. I was in jail, and you left. Can't compare the two."

That was kind of true. Teagan rubbed her hand up and down her opposite forearm. "Well, it's not too late, Reed. It's not too late to be this better person you're talking about. If that's who you want to be, you can."

He raised his gaze to find hers, those green eyes piercing through her. "And for us? Is it too late for us?"

She didn't want to answer that, but the little voice in the back of her head already seemed to know the answer. Slowly, Teagan nodded her head. "So much has happened, Reed. I just...I don't see how. I'm here now. My life is here. And you? You've got a lot to figure out."

Reed looked crestfallen, but not surprised. His throat bobbed as he swallowed. "You're right. I do. I'm sorry, Teag."

"I know you are," she replied, closing the gap between them again. She wrapped her arms around his neck, giving him a tight hug.

Reed's arms circled her waist, pulling her into his body and burying his face in her neck. "I'm so sorry," he repeated, this time his voice cracking. "I should have been there. I should have been the man you deserved."

She hugged him tighter, rubbing his back. "You will be one day. For someone."

"For you," Reed said, pulling away just enough to look her in the eyes. His were rimmed red, and his jaw was set. "I know we're in different places in our lives right now, but that's temporary."

"Reed..."

He shook his head, pulling her tighter against his body. "No. It's my turn to talk. I made a mistake once. Hell, a million times. But falling in love with you? That's the only thing I've ever done right." Reed slid his hand behind her head and kissed her softly. "If I have to, I'll spend the rest of my life trying to become the man you deserve."

Teagan's chest throbbed, as if she could actually feel her heart breaking as they kissed. She let him pull her closer, their tongues dancing as they kissed passionately. It was both a goodbye and a declaration of love all in one.

Sliding her hands down his chest, she moved to his belt

buckle and began pulling at it. There was a desperation building inside her, and she suddenly needed him now more than ever—even if it was their last time. "Reed..."

He growled against her neck, nipping her skin as he helped her release his cock from his pants. Reed grabbed her by her hips, lifting her against him. She wrapped her legs around him and let him carry her to the long, velvet couch to one end of the dressing room. The moment her back hit the cushions, she was wiggling out of her skirt. He climbed between her legs and pressed inside her almost immediately.

Teagan groaned and arched her back, curling into his brick-wall-like chest. "Oh, God."

"Fuck, Teag," he whispered huskily in her ear. "You're so wet."

She lifted her hips to meet his, moving in rhythm with his thrusts. There was no way she could even focus on why she was doing this right now, but all she knew was that the sadness was too much. It was too painful, and for just a few minutes, she wanted to feel good. She wanted them to make each other feel good—take from each other one last time before the door on their love closed for good.

An ache pounded in her chest at the thought, and tears stung her eyes.

The dressing room began to splinter around her as she began trembling with the pressure building inside her. She'd never been so full of pleasure and grief all at the same time, but when her climax hit her, she pressed into Reed's chest as he held her and finished inside her. He wrapped his arms around her back, holding her tightly as they stayed locked together.

She couldn't hold back her tears anymore, letting them slide down the sides of her face to her temples as her shoulders shook.

He gently caressed her hair, kissing her. "It'll be okay, Teag. It's okay."

"I love you, Reed," she admitted in halted sobs against his chest. "I've been in love with you for most of my life."

He placed a soft kiss against her lips. "I'm so in love with you, Teag. And I will be until the day I die."

"I'm sorry," she said, sniffing and trying to compose herself. "I'm sorry we couldn't make it work."

"Yet," Reed reminded her. "This isn't goodbye, Teag."

She smiled sadly at him, not wanting to be the one to take his hope away. But hers? It was gone—the pain between them too intense. The trust gone, fearing he'd never be the man she'd known he could be.

They'd had so many chances, and they'd still been unable to make it work.

They were over.

CHAPTER TWENTY-FOUR

"Um...what?" Jason blinked, staring across the desk at Reed. "You're what?"

"I'm taking a sabbatical." Reed lifted one leg, placing his ankle on the opposite knee, as he sat and stared at his agent. "So, you'll need to let the projects I've signed on to know."

Jason placed his elbows on the desk, steepling his fingers in front of his face. "Reed, I don't think you understand the money on the line here."

"I'll pay back any advance if the project can't wait until I get back."

He shook his head. "You realize that means I have to pay back my ten percent, too, right?"

"I'll pay your percent, too," Reed assured him. He certainly wasn't going to fuck over his agent just because he'd made his own decisions for his life. "This isn't me trying to destroy my career. I'm not quitting. I just need a break."

"What about *Break Down 2*?" Jason asked, already starting to write notes on his pad. "You can't pass on the sequel when you're the leading role."

Reed considered it for a moment. "When does shooting start?"

Jason opened his calendar on his phone. "Uh, two months after the premiere of the first movie."

"That's fine," Reed assured him. "I'll be back in time for the premiere."

Nothing was going to keep him from the event he'd see Teagan at.

Jason licked his lips, his jaw set tightly. "This is really fucking annoying, Scott."

"I'm sorry," he replied, though he wasn't actually sorry at all. He'd been working nonstop for eight years and raked in millions of dollars. He needed the break to step back and focus on himself, focus on growing as a person. How he was going to do that was still pretty unclear, but there was certainly no way to become a better person in Hollywood. He needed out, even if only for a little while. "But this will be a good thing in the long-term."

Reed pushed up to his feet, leaning over and offering a hand to Jason. "I'll see you in a couple months."

Jason shook his hand. "You might make me the most money, but you're my least favorite client, dickhead."

Reed laughed, his head tipping back. "You're my least favorite agent, asshole."

"Well, at least we're on the same page about something," Jason replied, grinning now. "Good luck on your sabbatical. I'm probably still going to blow up your phone."

"I'll probably turn it off," Reed teased, though he actually planned on doing just that. "See you later, man."

They shook hands one more time, and then Reed headed out of the office and toward his car. He glanced in the back seat of his car as he climbed in, checking that his suitcases were all still there. Between now and the movie premiere, he was going back to the one place where he felt truly him best self.

Thanks to Los Angeles traffic, it was almost two hours until he was pulling into the driveway. He parked his car and climbed out, taking his luggage out of the back seat and placing it on the asphalt.

The soft thunk of his car door closing was the announcement of Reed's fresh start. He paused and drew a deep breath, taking in the navy blue house with white shutters, surrounded by some kind of red flowering bushes and sitting pristinely in the center of a patch of just-mowed green grass. The white picket fence that encircled the whole thing was like icing on the cake of suburbia, a distant cry from the modern penthouses and bright lights of the city he'd just left behind. Sunlight flashed off the fire engine red front door as it swung wide open.

"Uncle Reed!" Nell came charging through the door, racing down the porch stairs and throwing herself into his arms.

"Ooof!" Reed pretended to groan at the onslaught, but it actually didn't hurt one bit. In fact, there was nothing he loved more than hugging his niece. "You almost knocked me over!"

"Well, I'm getting taller. Mom said I'm going to be taller than her one day," Nell said matter-of-factly.

Reed laughed. "That might be true. Your mom could fit in my pocket."

"Hey!" Penelope called out from where she was standing on the front porch. "I heard that!"

"Hey, shorty," Reed greeted her, laughing and walking up the walkway with a suitcase in one arm and Nell in the other. "Ready for your new roommate?"

She grinned. "I put some sheets on the couch. Your feet are probably going to hang off the edge, but you said that was fine."

"More than fine," he insisted, placing Nell on the ground and walking behind them into the house. "I don't need much. Just my family."

Penelope patted him on the back. "Well, you're officially my go-to babysitter, so you'll get a lot of that."

Reed smiled, more than fine with that as well. If there was one thing he wanted from this sabbatical, it was normalcy. He'd spent the last decade in search of fame and wealth, and none of it had made him happy. None of it had made him feel the way he felt when he was reading Nell a bedtime story or teasing his sister across the dinner table. No amount of money or attention made him feel whole.

But the way his family looked at him? That was more fulfilling than any red carpet or signing bonus.

While he'd sworn to win Teagan back one day, that wasn't why he was here. She was right—he wasn't ready. And he wanted to get ready, but not for her. For himself. He needed to find his center, his base—the place where he felt at home.

He had seen that in Teagan last week when he'd visited her in New York City. He'd seen that feeling of belonging that emanated just from her being surrounded by the lights and inspiration of Broadway. There was never a moment he'd felt that, or stopped and focused on finding that.

"So, what the heck are you doing here?" Penelope asked him as she sat down at the breakfast bar and sipped on her cup of coffee.

Reed glanced over at his niece, but Nell was in the living room already, playing on her iPad and oblivious to her conversation. "I just needed a break, you know?"

"A break from glitz and glamor?" Penelope snorted. "Wow, what a hard life you lead."

He grinned. "You know what I mean. I've been...I don't know. My priorities haven't been in the right place."

She raised one brow. "Uh, clearly. I'm the one who just bailed you out of jail, remember?"

"Little hard to forget five days behind bars," he assured her.

"What about Teagan?" Penelope prodded. "Have you spoken with her yet?"

He nodded, looking away for a moment. "We spoke."

"And?"

"And, it's over," he replied, exhaling loudly. "She doesn't want to continue things."

"Good for her." Penelope clapped her hands. "About time she kicked you to the curb."

Reed furrowed his brows. "Thanks, *sis*. Aren't you supposed to be on my side?"

"Uh, no one should be on your side right now." Penelope pushed her hair back over her shoulder. "But, yeah, I'm on your side. I just think you don't deserve her yet. She's practically an angel—she always was. You've got a lot of work to do before you deserve that."

"I'll never deserve her." Which was the truth. Despite the changes he wanted to make, he knew none of it would matter. She would always deserve better than him, and he was just going to have to except that. In the meantime, he was going to focus on himself. He was going to focus on being the man his family deserved—the uncle that Nell deserved.

"Well, you have us." Penelope stood, walked around the counter, and then embraced him around his waist. "We will always be here."

"Group hug!" Nell came running over and threw her arms around both of them.

Reed laughed, embracing his sister and niece in one go. Already he was beginning to feel at home; like this is exactly where he belonged. And for the next few months, this was exactly where he wanted to be.

CHAPTER TWENTY-FIVE

"How's BENSON liking New York City?" Simone tossed a small ball of yarn in the air and watched as Benson ran in circles on the wood floor trying to catch it.

Teagan leaned back into the couch, putting her feet up on the coffee table. "As long as there's a sunny spot, he doesn't care where he is."

"What about you?" Simone turned to her. "Still as dreamy as that first night?"

Teagan grinned. After almost two months in New York City, not a single ounce of the magic had worn off yet. "Even better," she replied. "I'm up for an understudy position for one of the bigger parts."

"Wait, so you're being promoted already?"

She shrugged. "Not really promoted. More like, I'd fill in if the current actress was sick."

"Then who takes your role?" Simone seemed confused, and granted, it could all get a little confusing but Teagan had quickly adapted to the fast-paced world of Broadway.

"Another understudy." Teagan tossed the yarn back toward

Benson after he'd batted it across the floor back to her. "So, basi-cally just switching us around."

"That sounds like a promotion."

She tried not to smile, but it was impossible to do anything but lately. "I guess it kind of is."

"Do you have any wine here?" Simone sat up and looked toward the kitchen.

Teagan shook her head. "Nope. Been on a strict diet since starting the show. No empty calories or I'm not going to fit in my costume."

"See, that's why I love singing." Simone picked up a magazine from the coffee table and started leafing through it. "No one cares if I have a muffin top as long as I can belt out those notes."

Teagan had long admired her younger sister's talent with the microphone. Simone's voice was strong and dynamic, and when she sang, Teagan got chills.

"Well, it's not only the show's fault," she replied, running a hand over her stomach. "Certain foods have been making me nauseous lately. I think I might have a gluten allergy, so I'm trying to give up particular foods until I figure out what's making me sick."

"Oh, that's even worse." Simone groaned. "There's nothing I love more than gluten."

"You probably don't even know what gluten is."

Simone chuckled. "I know it's probably something that makes food delicious."

Well, she wasn't wrong.

"When is your flight back to Los Angeles?" Simone asked her.

Teagan clicked the calendar app on her phone and scrolled through the next few weeks. "On the tenth. Two weeks from tomorrow."

"Mom's going to be ecstatic. She complains everyday about you being so far away."

Teagan scoffed. "I tried to buy her a ticket to come out here."
"You know Mom doesn't do planes."

She shrugged. "She's going to have to learn."

Simone let a beat go by before she put down the magazine and turned to face her. "Are you nervous?"

"For the premiere?" Teagan furrowed her brows. "I'm excited. A once-in-a-lifetime experience. Never been on a red carpet before except occasionally as Aria's date."

Her sister shook her head. "No, for seeing Reed. Walking the red carpet with him and all that. You won't be able to avoid him—hell, I doubt he'd even let you. That man is in love with you."

"No, he's not. We're over." She kept playing on her phone, trying not to think about the man who'd broken her heart twice and yet somehow still held it in his hands. "I made it very, very clear. He and I are done for good."

Simone scoffed. "Mmkay. But like, really, how are you going to act when you see him?"

"I'm going to be cordial and friendly. We're professionals, Simmy."

Her sister lifted one brow. "What about when you're off camera?"

"Exactly the same."

She was not going to let seeing Reed rile her, nor was she going to let him ruin her night. As much as she was in love with Broadway, she had seriously enjoyed her role in *Break Down* and if she ever had the chance to do another movie, she would take it.

She hated to admit it, but the fame was exciting. Her upcoming role in the movie was already being touted by critics as a break-out role, and, while the tabloid article had been a huge invasion of privacy, the leak about her and Reed had catapulted her into the public's eyes. Actual paparazzi followed her around on occasion now, her social media followers were in the hundreds of thousands, and reporters called her frequently for interviews.

She never told them anything, of course, but it seemed that the quieter she was, the more they wanted her.

None of this had ever been about the perks—the money or the fame—but now having both, she was definitely enjoying it. The movie paycheck, along with what she was making from the show, was more money than she'd ever seen in her life, and for the first time, she actually felt like she didn't need anyone else.

She'd earned this role based on her talent and her hard work, after years of almost losing everything from that car accident. Climbing her way back to the top, she'd achieved more than she thought possible, and she was finally giving herself credit for it. She didn't need help or a leg up from anyone—she did this on her own and she would keep doing this on her own.

When she looked back on it, she wondered if that had been a contributing issue to her first breakup with Reed. Hell, maybe even their second, too. She'd been so willing to give up her dreams to marry him—to depend on him. She'd completely sacrificed herself, and he hadn't even asked her to. Maybe it was fear, maybe it was something else, but either way, that had been a mistake.

For the first time in her life, she was putting herself first. Her dreams, her wants, her needs. It was exhilarating, and she was realizing just how much she'd put herself on the back burner before. But it wasn't just that she'd put her needs to the side— she'd been afraid to put herself first. Following her dreams, going after what she wanted...that meant she had more to lose.

Chasing success also meant she could fail.

That was a fear she had struggled with all her life. Being the supportive best friend, the encouraging younger sister, the cheering choreographer on the sidelines—none of it put her in the spotlight. None of it put the responsibilities on her shoulders. She couldn't fail.

Now, on a Broadway stage in a prominent role? Damn, could

she fail, and fail hard. But she wasn't. Every day she worked harder and harder to be the best she could be in her role, and every day it showed.

"Well, I think it won't be as easy as you're pretending it will be," Simone continued. "I know you two are 'over' or whatever, but I see the way your eyes light when his name comes up."

"Simmy, just because someone is your first love, doesn't mean they'll be your last."

She shrugged. "I've never been in love, so what do I know? I just think you two are good together."

Teagan scoffed, staring at her sister. "Literally a few months ago you were acting like I was insane to date him again."

"You definitely were insane," Simone agreed. "But from what I've heard, that's what love is. Fucking crazy."

She laughed, tipping her head back. "Okay, you have a point there."

Simone tapped the side of her head. "I know things sometimes."

"Either way, it truly is over. I'll love Reed forever because he was a huge part of my life, he was everything to me for years." Teagan swallowed at the thought. Grief still came in waves, because just when she thought she was getting over him, the longing would hit and she'd be sad again. "But we're moving on. I've moved on. Our lives are going different directions."

"Technically, I think his life is on pause." Simone yawned, the late-night hour clearly starting to affect her. "I heard he quit acting."

Teagan furrowed her brow. "Really? Where did you hear that?"

"Mom. She said he's apparently gone MIA, and the tabloids are all speculating as to where he is." Simone picked up Benson and began cuddling him, despite his annoyance with her decision. "Some people think he's in rehab."

"He didn't have a drug problem," Teagan replied. "I rarely saw him drink, either."

"Well, he got arrested for that drunken brawl."

Teagan shook her head. "He'd barely had a couple drinks that night."

"Maybe he should have had more." Simone chuckled. "Sorry."

Teagan didn't reply, but she couldn't stop wondering where Reed was or why he'd fallen off the pop culture map. Part of her wanted to reach out, ask him if he was okay, but that would open a door she'd been firmly trying to close for months.

"He'll be at the premiere," she assured Simone. "He wouldn't miss it."

Too many people would be depending on him to be there. Whatever he was doing or whatever he was going through, she just knew in her gut that he wouldn't do anything to disappoint the cast and crew, let alone his fans. Despite his antics in the press, she'd seen how hard he cared for his craft and how kindly he treated fans.

"He wouldn't miss seeing you," Simone replied. "Guaranteed."

Teagan chuckled and rolled her eyes. "Let. It. Go."

Simone grinned. "Fiiiine, but when you all eventually have babies, name your firstborn daughter after me."

Oh, shit. A sense of dread rolling through her, Teagan grabbed for her cell phone, quickly pulling the calendar app back up. She scrolled through the past two months, looking for any reminder that she hadn't just made a giant mistake.

Nothing. There was nothing.

"Simone..." Teagan's eyes widened as she turned to her sister. "We need to run an errand."

"It's late," Simone whined, kicking her feet up onto the coffee table.

"We need to go now, Simmy!" Teagan was already standing and pulling on her jacket as she shouted. "Come on!"

"What the hell?" Simone jumped up, looking startled. "Christ, what's the matter?"

Teagan paused at the door and looked at her. "I think I'm pregnant."

Simone's mouth fell open. "*Oh, shit.*"

CHAPTER TWENTY-SIX

"ARE YOU BACK FROM PURGATORY OFFICIALLY?" Jason walked right into the Reed's penthouse the moment he'd opened the door.

"I just came home yesterday," Reed confirmed, closing the door behind him. "How'd you know?"

Jason shrugged and headed for the bar cart, opening a bottle of scotch. "Paid off your doorman to keep me updated."

"Of course you did." Reed rolled his eyes. "That's not an invasion of privacy at all."

"Privacy is a privilege." Jason took a sip and coughed lightly. "Damn, that's good shit. Want a glass?"

Reed shook his head. While he'd never had a problem with drinking, he'd certainly partaken in enough in his lifetime to warrant a break. With his hiatus, he'd focused on health and mindfulness, getting back to his roots. It had been an amazing two months with his sister and niece, and then welcoming his brother-in-law home from deployment.

He'd spent the last decade running from normalcy. Running from everything he thought would hold him back, would suffocate his freedom and his dreams. Ironically, living his life like that had only made him more lost than ever before.

Running back home, back to white picket fences...it was the first time he'd felt *found*.

"So, I've got news," Jason began, settling into a leather arm chair in his living room. "The script for *Break Down 2* was overhauled."

Reed took a seat in a chair across from him. "Really? Why?"

"Elena got a spot on *Dancing with the Starlets*," he explained. "She doesn't want to do the sequel."

"Oh, damn. That's a great gig." Reed furrowed his brows. "So, what does this mean for the sequel? The entire first movie was about our love story."

"They killed her off. The movie starts with you being sad and in mourning, along with her best friend who's also grieving. You two then fall in love through mutual grief or some shit like that. Plus, a crapload of dancing and mushy ass scenes."

That didn't sound like a terrible plot, actually. "Well, I'm in. Sounds stronger than the first draft of the script, actually."

Jason nodded his head. "Honestly, it is infinitely better. But, that leaves us with a problem."

Reed furrowed his brow. "What?"

"The best friend..." Jason gestured with his hands, as if to try and catch him up.

Fuck. "Teagan." He suddenly realized what Jason was getting at. "I'm supposed to do an entire love story with my ex-fiancée."

"I mean, it's actually marketing gold," his agent continued. "Fans know your history and they'll eat that shit up. The producers are hammering for it, because they think it's a fantastic angle."

Reed could see why the executives behind the camera would think that, but they'd never stood on a mark and had to stare at the woman they still loved.

Jason continued, "But, can you handle it?"

"I think so." Reed rubbed his hand across the back of his neck. "I mean, I'm going to have to."

"Reluctant compliance—that's the spirit!" Jason slapped his shoulder in solidarity. "You two will be great on camera. The chemistry is still there, I'm sure."

He exhaled loudly. "That's probably true. Does Teagan know about the script change yet?"

Jason shook his head. "Not yet, but I'm working on negotiating her contract now."

"I hope you're getting her everything she deserves," Reed warned.

"First of all, I'm the best fucking agent in town," Jason reminded him. "And, second, your girl is blowing up. Her value has skyrocketed to production companies, so don't worry—she's going to make bank."

Reed grinned, a sense of pride warming him. It was a new feeling for him—caring so much about someone else's success. He wanted to call her up right now and congratulate her on everything she's accomplished.

Unfortunately, that wasn't an option. She'd made it very clear that they were over.

He wasn't sure if he was excited or dreading seeing her at the movie premiere in two days. Every glimpse of her was pure joy, but knowing she wanted nothing to do with him was excruciating. He wondered if he was even capable of handling that roller coaster.

"I'm glad you're taking care of her," Reed replied.

"Speaking of you and Teagan," Jason started, refilling his glass of scotch. "I think you two should meet up before the premiere to discuss all of this."

"What? Why?" There was no way he was doing that.

"I know you can both be professional, but I still think clearing the air before a shit ton of cameras are pointing at you would be a good idea." Jason knocked back his second glass of scotch, hissing as it went down rough. "Maybe avoid a public relations nightmare or something like that. But what do I know."

Reed considered his advice, but it still seemed like dangerous territory. She'd made her wishes very clear. "I'll think about it."

Which was the truth. It was impossible *not* to think about her. He'd taken the last two months to himself, and really worked on who he was and who he wanted to be. But that didn't mean he wasn't thinking about her or trying to become the man she deserved to be with. Even if she never took him back, he wanted to be the man he saw reflected in her eyes. The way she looked at him with such faith and pride in who he was—he wanted to be the man who deserved that. Not just for her, but for himself.

"But, um..." Jason swirled the ice in his glass. "It wouldn't be the worst thing in the world if you two patched things up."

Reed's eyes widened and he stared at his agent in surprise. "Are you serious? Wasn't it you who told me to stay away from her a few months ago? Made me promise *no* women? Didn't you even get her a job across the country to separate us?"

Jason nodded. "Yeah—that was then. This is now. And now? Teagan's star cred is blowing up, and if you two join forces, this next movie will, too. Plus, the other deals and endorsements we could get for the second-chance-lovers-who-made-it-work-against-all-odds would be an insane amount of cash."

Of course it was about the money. "I'm not going to date someone for a paycheck."

"That's not what I'm saying," Jason clarified. "But if it were to organically happen...that'd be great for everyone."

Reed wished it would organically happen, but he wasn't holding his breath.

"And imagine if you knocked her up?" Jason laughed, pouring more scotch. "Oh, good Lord, we'd be rolling in millions."

Reed rolled his eyes. "Maybe you should stop drinking because you sound insane now."

"Dead serious, Reed. I don't joke about money."

"I'll talk to her—but that's it. No babies." Reed stood from his chair and went in search of his cell phone. "Like I'm even ready to be a dad. I can't even imagine."

CHAPTER TWENTY-SEVEN

"That no-good, goddamn, motherfucking piece of shit!" Teagan's Father, Jack Reynolds, tossed his empty beer can into the trash can in a high arc, landing squarely in the center.

"Dad!" Teagan chided. "That's a little harsh, don't you think?"

"Not harsh enough," Teagan's mother, Betty, replied. "If you ask me, I'd slap the beard off his chin."

Her father angled his wheelchair to face her. After years battling multiple sclerosis, he'd been forced to spend the rest of his life in an non-ambulatory state. "Baby girl, you've got to see it from our perspective. First, we paid for a wedding he didn't come to."

"Not that it's about the money," her mother chimed in.

Her father continued, "Second, we were with you every day during your recovery."

"Where was he? Huh?" Her mother was basically her father's commentary.

"And, third, now you're telling me that my beautiful, virginal baby girl..."

"I mean, virginal is a stretch, Jack," her mother decided to add.

Teagan rolled her eyes. "Mom. Seriously?"

Her father was not deterred. "My beautiful baby girl is now pregnant with that man's child?"

"Gee, Dad. Why don't you tell me how you really feel?" Teagan ran her hands over her stomach, still absorbing the news herself. It had been two weeks since she'd peed on a stick in front of Simone and seen the positive sign. She'd immediately seen her doctor and started on prenatal vitamins and all that, but the shock was still there.

One moment of quick goodbye sex on a dressing room couch could really throw a wrench in things.

"Ooh, this is so exciting!" Her mother clapped her hands with excitement. "My second grandchild. I can't even believe it!"

"I'm confused," Teagan interrupted, feeling like she was on a roller coaster ride. She'd come home to Los Angeles for the movie premiere and finally told her parents the news. Honestly, she was surprised Simone and Aria had both been able to keep quiet about it, because they had been the first to know but Teagan had insisted on telling their parents in person. "Are you guys happy or angry?"

Her father grinned. "About having another grandchild? Fucking ecstatic!" He reached forward and rubbed her belly. "Sorry you have a shit dad, little peanut."

"Jack! Don't say that," her mother scolded him, pushing him away. She got close to Teagan's stomach and placed her hand against her. "Little Peanut, your grandfather is very old and very grumpy and we don't listen to anything he says."

Teagan laughed, but then pushed everyone off her stomach. "Good Lord, guys. Boundaries. I'm only ten weeks."

"I can see him already," her mother pointed. "You're going to pop early."

She smiled and looked down at her stomach, actually excited to see it grow for the first time in her life. As unexpected as this was, and as untimely as it was with her plans, she had fallen in love the moment she saw that tiny little heartbeat on the monitor. It was a new feeling of adoration and obsession and love and protectiveness she'd never even known was possible before.

"What are you going to do about your show?" Jack asked. "Can your cat be a pregnant cat?"

"Surprisingly, yes," Teagan replied, remembering the conversation with her director. "Until the point where a doctor says it's unsafe, I can keep dancing. The costume actually covers me pretty well, so it won't be hard to hide."

"And *Break Down* 2 will be wrapped within two or three months, so you shouldn't be showing too much by then," her mother added. "We'll try and get them to move up the filming date, but they were already pushing for that, so it shouldn't be an issue."

"A well-placed plant, or carefully positioned purse, and you won't even see my stomach."

Her father nodded, clearly still trying to absorb all the information. "And what about the rat bastard?"

"Dad, I swear to God, if you keep insulting the father of my child..."

He put his hands up. "Fine. Fine. What about the angelic chorus boy whose child you are cooking up in there?"

"Gross. I think I liked the cussing better." Teagan sighed as she thought about Reed and what she was going to do about telling him. "I honestly have no idea. We're supposed to meet for lunch tomorrow to—as my agent says—*patch things up* before the premiere. I guess he's afraid we'll fight on camera or something."

"Fight, make love—it's really all the same thing." Her mother leaned down and kissed Jack on the top of his head. "But you're going to have to tell him."

"I will tell him," she assured them. There was no way she'd hide something like this from him. Just because they weren't going to work out as a couple didn't mean he didn't have a right to be in his child's life. Now they were just going to have to figure out what that looked like. "But probably after the premiere. It might be awkward, otherwise."

Betty shrugged her shoulders. "Honestly, is it ever not awkward to tell your ex-twice-boyfriend that you're accidentally carrying his baby?"

"Christ. I walked in at a weird moment," Simone said, having just entered the living room of their parent's house where they were sitting. "Oh, you told them!" She clapped her hands, then paused. "Wait...did I miss a 'rat bastard'? That's my favorite dad-ism."

Teagan laughed. "It's one of the first things he said."

Simone high-fives her father. "You never disappoint, Pops."

"I am pretty impressive," he joked, using a funny voice to mimic a movie quote. "Oh, we also named the baby, Simmy."

"Uh, if it's a girl, I hope it's named Simone." She struck a pose, pointing to herself. "Actually, if it's a boy, I'm fine with that, too."

"Peanut," Betty replied. "Little Peanut."

"What a nutty name," Jack teased then mimicked the sound of a rim shot on drums. "Ba dum shh!"

They continued to joke and laugh, and Teagan sat back to watch them and take it all in. She ran her hand in small circles over her belly. *I love you, little peanut. And I apologize in advance that this is the family you're going to be born into.*

I didn't ask for them either.

CHAPTER TWENTY-EIGHT

REED PICKED his napkin up off the table and spread it across his lap. It didn't look right. He picked it up, unfolded it until it was flat, then smoothed it out again across his lap. His foot bounced and he straightened the silverware next to his plate.

"Hey."

His gaze lifted, and he took in the beautiful woman who'd just approached his table. She was every bit as gorgeous as she'd always been, and even though they'd been apart a few short months, it suddenly felt like forever. There was something different about her now—lighter, happier.

Half of him wanted to celebrate for her, thrilled she'd clearly found something—or someone—who made her glow the way she currently was. She deserved that peace and joy. But, there was a darker half of him that wanted her to have missed him, to have not flourished apart from him. All the more reason why she had been right—they weren't good for each other.

Or, rather, he wasn't good for her.

Reed stood quickly and pulled out her chair. "Hey, Teag."

"Thank you," she replied, sitting in the offered seat and tucking her own napkin on her lap.

He took his seat across from her and tried for a smile. "So... how have you been?"

She nodded slowly. "I've been really good, actually. The show is...it's amazing. It's everything I ever dreamed of for my career."

"That's wonderful, Teag," he replied, and he genuinely meant it. "You worked hard for that role."

Her cheeks reddened slightly at that, a small smile at the corner of her lips. "I did. Thank you." She played with the edge of her plate, fidgeting slightly. "And you? How have you been?"

Reed leaned back slightly. "I took the last few months off, so the break has been really nice."

"Mmm, I heard." A nervousness passed over her expression. "Was it...well, the papers were saying it was rehab?"

He laughed louder than he'd meant to, then calmed himself. "No. Nothing like that. I just stayed with my sister in the suburbs for two months. Took care of Nell. Slept on a couch half my size. It was a great time."

Teagan's brows furrowed, but she was smiling. "You did? *You?*"

"Yes, me." He put his hand to his chest. "I was trying something new. Something...normal."

"And how did you like the...normal?"

He grinned. "White picket fences aren't so bad."

Pain met her eyes for a moment then was gone. "I told you."

"You did."

They were both silent for a moment, and then the waiter thankfully interrupted them to take their orders.

"So," Reed began after the waiter had dropped back off his glass of wine and Teagan's soda—which was a bit odd, because he'd never seen her drink soda before. "Have you spoken to Jason lately?"

"About *Break Down 2?*" Teagan nodded. "He told me yesterday."

"Are you going to take the role?" He suddenly realized how badly he wanted her to say yes. It wasn't just that he wanted to film a love story with her, it was that he wanted to spend every day by her side. He wanted to go to work and have her be there.

Hell, he wanted to come home and have her be there, too.

"I'm still negotiating terms, trying to move up the filming date, but...yes." She nodded slowly, chewing on the edge of her lip in a way that made him more turned on than he'd like to admit in the middle of a busy lunch hour at a popular restaurant. "I think so. It'll be an amazing career opportunity for me."

"Move up the filming?" He'd already moved it back when he'd taken his few months off, though he didn't mind it moving up now that he was back. "Why's that? Do you have another gig?"

Teagan's face twitched, like she was trying to hide a smile. Finally, it broke free and she grinned. "Yeah. The role of a life-time. I'm really excited."

He lifted one brow. "That sounds amazing. Tell me about it."

"Maybe soon." She went back to chewing on her bottom lip. "Soon."

The waiter delivered their food, and for another minute or two, they were quiet as they both enjoyed their dishes. Finally, Reed put down his fork and looked at her. "Why is this so awkward?"

She looked startled at his admission. "I'm...I'm not sure. It doesn't feel like it should be, but we're so forced."

Reed moved his plate to the side and reached across the table to squeeze her hand. "Teag, I know what you said, and I don't want to push things, but I also can't stop what I'm feeling."

"Reed, don't do this." She looked away, but she didn't move her hand from his. "We're supposed to just be civil and catch up before the premiere tomorrow."

"I've never done what I'm supposed to do, and so here we are," Reed replied, this time standing and switching to the chair directly next to hers. He angled his knees to be on either side of hers, pulling her chair closer to him. "These last two months were good for me. I needed them. I needed them apart from you."

She looked up at him, surprise in her dark brown eyes.

"But that doesn't mean I didn't think about you every day," he continued. "I am so sorry I messed up our second chance with that arrest, but I need you to know I want a third. And when I mess that one up, I want a fourth. And a fifth, and a sixth."

Tears brimmed her lower lashes, but she kept her gaze on their hands clutched together between them.

"I've made a lot of mistakes, Teag, but falling in love with you is not one of them." He carefully pushed a piece of her hair behind her ear. "And whether it's eight years apart or two months, I'm in love with you, Teagan. I always will be."

A flash in the corner of his eye caught him off guard. He looked to see several restaurant patrons had their phones out and were taking pictures of what probably looked like a romantic, intimate moment between lovers.

Teagan's eyes widened. "We should get out of here."

"Agreed." He grabbed a few bills out of his wallet and put them down on the table. Grabbing her hand, he led them out of the restaurant and made the first turn down an alleyway.

She looked confused, but he stepped closer to her, backing her against the brick wall until he had her pinned. Her chest began rising and falling faster as his lips hovered over hers.

"Teagan...tell me you feel the same way." His palm slid down her neck, cupping her jaw as his thumb gentle caressed her cheek. "Tell me you're as in love with me today as you ever were."

"Reed, I told you two months ago that there was no hope left here," she reminded him, though her expression didn't match her words. "I...I told you."

"And I told you that I was going to do anything I could to bring you back to me."

She swallowed hard, placing her hand against his chest. "Things are different now, Reed. I have other...responsibilities...to think about."

Reed shook his head. "Teag, if you want to look for a reason for us not to be together, you're going to find one. But I'm here now, and I'm telling you that I'm ready to devote everything I am and everything I have to you. Hell, I'd marry you right now. Let's go find a chapel and make it official. You're it for me."

A small smile lifted the corners of her lips. "Reed, don't be ridiculous."

"No part of me is joking," he replied, lowering his lips to hers again. He brushed against her gently, waiting for that hitch in her breath that told him she wanted this as badly as he did.

Then, there it was, that tiny gasp as she leaned into him. Her breasts pushed against his chest, and he tried to ignore them, but really all he wanted was to pull off her shirt right then and there and have her nipples in his mouth. His mind was playing tricks on him because he was almost sure they seemed bigger than before.

His lips pressed against hers, a soft moan escaping her and allowing his tongue to slide inside her mouth. Their bodies pressed tighter together, a frantic feeling coming over him at how desperately he needed her right then and there. He wanted to hitch up her skirt and plunge inside her right in this alleyway.

He growled in her ear. "Fuck, Teag..."

"Not here." She shook her head. "Not now. I...I have something to show you first."

"Please tell me it's you naked and stretched out across my bed."

Teagan giggled—literally giggled. He'd never seen her do that before. Hell, he'd never seen her this happy before. "It's not that. But kinda naked-body-related."

"I'm intrigued. Where to?" He pulled his car keys out of his pocket and directed them back onto the sidewalk and in the direction of his car.

"It's about ten minutes away," she replied. "I'll tell you how to get there when we're in the car."

He frowned, but decided not to push further. She was a different version of the Teagan he knew—more confident, happier, and more take-charge. He liked it, and if it would bring her back to him, he was all for whatever she was about to show him.

CHAPTER TWENTY-NINE

WHAT THE HELL am I doing? Teagan sat nervously in the passenger seat of Reed's car as she tried to come up with some explanation for why she'd lost her damn mind.

"Turn right, and then it's that parking lot up there," she instructed him.

He eased the car into a parking spot and then put it in park. "An office building?"

"You'll see." She climbed out of the car, and the moment they were by each other again, he took her hand. She didn't stop him, and she didn't pull away. She couldn't.

She didn't want to.

Trying to resist his advances over lunch had been the most excruciating thing she'd ever done, but she didn't want him to make any decisions until he knew the full truth. Learning about his last few months, and seeing the difference in his demeanor and spirit, it was everything she'd one hoped for from him. He was calmer, gentler, and there was a contentment in him that she'd honestly never thought she'd see.

It was like he'd finally stopped running and embraced the

demons that had been chasing him. And maybe they weren't demons at all.

It was no wonder why she wanted to throw her arms around his neck and tell him how much she loved him, too. Because despite her constant denouncements and their multiple breakups, she felt exactly the same today as she did the first time she saw him walking toward her across the quad in college.

But he needed to know what he was signing up for. He needed the full picture.

She walked him into the building and down a back hallway, then quickly ushered him into an office before he could look around.

"Ms. Reynolds," the receptionist greeted her. "Oh, and Mr. Scott." The older woman blushed deeply, like she had a secret, and suddenly Teagan wondered if this was a good idea.

"Is Dr. Natividad available for a moment?"

She nodded furiously. "Of course, of course. I'll go get her now. If you want to head back to the first exam room, she'll meet you there."

"'Teag," Reed lowered his voice. "What's going on?"

She put a finger to her lips and led him back to the exam room. Small and humble, the room didn't boast more than the necessary medical equipment. She hopped up onto the table, watching the emotions and confusion pass over his face.

"I don't understand." He was looking around the room for a clue. "Are you sick? Are you hurt? Is it your leg? None of this changes how I feel, Teagan. If that's why you're showing me this —it changes nothing."

Her heart melted at his words, and when he leaned in to kiss her again, she held on a little longer.

"Ahem," the doctor cleared her throat, and they quickly pulled apart. "Hi there, Ms. Reynolds. Mr. Scott, I presume?"

"Hey, doc." He shook her hand. "I've got to admit, I'm a little out of the loop here."

The doctor looked at Teagan for clarification.

"Is it—I mean, can we show him?" she replied, the hints of a smile pulling on her lips.

The doctor grinned. "I think we can make that happen."

She pulled a monitor over close to the exam table and settled into a chair.

Teagan lay down flat then lifted her shirt. The doctor squeezed some gel onto her stomach, then pushed a wand against her slightly swollen abdomen. A loud noise came through the speakers—*ba dum ba dum ba dum ba dum ba dum.*

Reed's eyes widened as he looked at the screen, then down at her. "Teag?"

She smiled, unable to hold back her excitement.

His jaw tensed and relaxed as he obviously struggled for words. "Teag, are you pregnant?" he finally managed to get out. "Are...are *we* pregnant?"

Teagan slowly nodded her head, but the moment she confirmed it, he threw his arms around her and they almost toppled off the table. "Reed!"

"I'll give you two a minute alone," Dr. Natividad said with a smile as she left the exam room.

"I'm sorry." He quickly righted them, tears streaming down his face. "I just..."

"Are you crying?" She wiped the tears from his cheeks with her thumb.

"Happy—so fucking happy—tears." He kissed her again, harder this time, and his tears mixed with hers. "Holy shit, Teag. We're going to be parents." Suddenly he paused. "Oh, damn it. Jason's going to be fucking thrilled. I hate making that fucker happy."

Teagan laughed, holding on to his shoulders for support since he was bouncing them all over the place.

"Babe, I know I said that falling in love with you was the best thing I ever did, but that was wrong." Reed shook his head, then pointed toward the image on the ultrasound of their baby. "This... This baby is the best thing I'll ever do in my entire life. Teagan, this is the most amazing thing you could have ever done for me."

"Uh, I didn't do this." She laughed, standing from the exam table and wiping the gel off her stomach. "You did this in my dressing room when you didn't use a condom."

"Fine, I'll take the credit. Go, Reed. You're killing it at life, man." He pretended to pat himself on the back, and she just laughed harder.

She offered him her hand. "Come on. Let's go home."

"Yeah? Whose home?" He kissed the back of her hand as they walked down the hallway and into the waiting room.

"I've been staying with my parents until I find a place big enough for the baby and me out here for when I'm filming *Break Down 2*. I'm still keeping my apartment in New York and plan to go back and forth until I can't fly anymore. Or, at least, that was the plan." Teagan glanced sideways at him. "I'm not...I mean, I don't know...do you still want this? This is basically an insta-white-picket-fence family, and I just don't know if you're ready for that. Do you still want all the things you said at lunch now that you know?"

He squeezed her hand. "I want it more."

She wanted to believe him. But how many times had she believed him before?

Teagan noticed a woman in the waiting room surreptitiously lifting her phone and aiming the camera in her direction. She quickly ducked her head, but it was probably a dead giveaway that she had one hand on her stomach, and the other hand in Reed's...in a gynecologist's office.

"You know this is about to become front page news, right?" Reed whispered to her, leaning in closer.

Teagan chuckled. "I really should have re-thought this whole tell-him-with-an-ultrasound plan."

He shrugged, opening the front door for her as they headed for his car across the parking lot. "I kind of like it. Let everyone know." He cupped his hand by his mouth and started shouting. "The love of my life is having my baby!"

"Oh, my, God! Reed!" She put her hand over his mouth, trying to muffle him. They were both laughing too hard to do any sort of damage control. "You're going to get us in so much trouble."

As much as she loved hearing that he cared for her, and how happy he was, her heart was trying to put on the brakes. This man in front of her was incredibly different from any version of him she'd met before. She barely recognized this Reed. There was no doubt in her mind that he'd taken a lot of time over the last few months to reevaluate his life, and she felt a sense of pride in him knowing he'd been strong enough to do so much work on himself.

"Are you kidding? Jason's going to be fucking thrilled. He's going to be planning how to make money off Peanut the moment he finds out." Reed growled, suddenly looking protective. "Don't worry. I won't let him."

When they got to the car, he went to open the door for her, but then paused. Pressing her back against the car, he kissed her again. "Tell me now," he urged. "Now that I know, and there are no secrets left...tell me where we are."

Teagan inhaled slowly. "I can't Reed. I just can't say it yet."

As badly as she wanted to tell him that she loved him—she'd never stopped—and that she wanted to make them work, her fear held her back. *Fool me once, shame on you. Fool me twice, shame on me.* She wasn't going to be the woman who went for a third time.

Reed pulled her tighter against him, his hand stretched over her stomach. "We'll get there."

She nodded, letting him kiss her because, God, there was nothing better than how his lips felt against hers. Now she just had to figure out a way to open her heart and trust he wouldn't break it...again.

CHAPTER THIRTY

"Can you tell?" Teagan turned her body to the side and smoothed her hand over her belly. "This dress is practically a second skin."

Reed grinned, having loved every minute of watching her get dressed for the movie premiere. Her dress was floor length and gold sequins that shimmered around her, elegant and breathtaking. He could stare at her all night—though he was seriously considering stripping the dress from her right then and there.

"I think you should move in with me," he said, instead of answering her original question.

Her eyes met his, a startled expression on her face. "What?"

"Move in with me. Marry me." He took her hand and pulled her against him, letting his fingers trail down her bare back where the dress dipped low. "We're together, so let's be together."

Teagan slid her tongue across her bottom lip, then shook her head. "You've lost your mind. It's too soon, Reed. We shouldn't even be having this conversation."

"I've known you for over a decade—how is that too soon?"

"That doesn't count, and you know it." Teagan stepped back

toward the mirror and began putting on her earrings. "We're not going to get married just because we're having a baby."

"I'm with you because I love you, Teag."

The corners of her lips twitched into the hint of a smile. "Then there's nothing to worry about. We'll get there. Eventually."

"I have to be honest," he said, rubbing the back of his neck and trying not to think about the diamond ring burning a hole in his pocket. He'd planned to propose to her later at the premiere, really make it romantic and special, but when he'd seen her just then...rubbing her hands over her belly, gorgeous in that dress. He hadn't been able to help himself. He'd needed to ask her right then and there. "I really didn't expect you to turn me down."

"Now you know what it feels like," she replied, chuckling and tossing a makeup sponge at him.

He grinned, glad that they were in a place that they could joke about his mistakes early on in their relationship. "That's cold, woman."

She shrugged, now placing a diamond necklace around her neck and then touching up the last of her makeup. "Are you almost ready to go?"

"I've been ready." He waved his hands down the length of his body—a classic tuxedo that fit him perfectly. "Unless you want to take it off and start over."

Teagan flashed him a teasing smile. "Think you have another round in you?"

"Without a doubt." He leaned in and kissed her softly, taking care not to smudge her makeup. "Come on. The limo is waiting."

She took his hand and then grabbed her clutch in the other. "Do you think this is a good idea? Showing up together?"

"Babe, have you seen the headlines today?"

Teagan shook her head. "I've been in a fitting since early this morning."

Reed pulled his phone out of his pocket and scrolled to TMZ. Handing it to her, he watched her expression as she looked at the top story on their page.

"Ugh." She groaned. "That was fast."

"I'd say the cat's out of the bag, Teag," he stated.

"Thank God my family already knows. They'd be so pissed if this is how they found out," Teagan mused, handing him back his phone.

"Oh, shit." Reed's eyes widened. "I should probably call my sister."

Teagan grimaced. "Oops."

"The moment the premiere's over, I'll tell her." Reed took her hand again, leading her out the front door and to the waiting limo. They climbed inside and settled on the backseat cuddled into one another.

"How's my favorite Hollywood power couple?" Jason turned around to look at them from the front seat. "We should talk."

"What the hell are you doing here, Jason?" Reed's brow furrowed as Jason climbed out of the passenger seat and came around to join them in the back.

"Scoot over," he instructed.

Reed and Teagan acquiesced, though neither were happy about it.

"So, first of all, thanks for keeping me in the loop about your big baby reveal to the world." Jason's sarcasm was thick, but his excitement was still easy to see.

"It wasn't really a planned moment," Teagan defended herself, placing a hand over her stomach. She was barely show-ing, but now that he knew, Reed was acutely aware of the slightly rounded swell of her belly.

"Fair enough," Jason replied. "But, second, now we need to plan what you're going to say. The reporters on the red carpet are going to be all over this story."

"We can just say we're in love and having a baby." Reed shrugged his shoulders. "Seems simple enough."

"Nope. You've got to add the movie in there—promote the fuck out of it. Say you fell in love on camera, and this baby is a direct result of *Break Down*."

"Ew." Teagan grimaced this time. "That sounds weird."

"Driver!" Reed called out to the front, rolling down the barricade between them. "Can you stop the car?"

The driver slowed the limo, still only a few feet out of his driveway.

"Call a cab, Jason." Reed opened the door for him. "We're going alone on this one. The only third party needed in this relationship is our baby."

Jason rolled his eyes. "Don't be dramatic, Reed."

"Seriously. Out." Reed pointed toward the open door.

Jason's nostrils flared and he exhaled loudly. "Fine, but we're meeting Monday to talk baby endorsements."

"No, we're not," Reed called out after his retreating figure as he climbed out of the car. There was no way he was going to use his future child as a money-making machine, nor was he going to let anyone else do that either. Reed closed the car door behind him. "Driver, you can continue. Thank you."

Teagan's hand was in front of her lips, but it was clear she was smiling and trying not to laugh.

"What?" he asked.

She shook her head. "I'm just so glad someone finally stood up to him." She was laughing now. "His face was priceless."

Reed couldn't help but chuckle as well. "I mean, he's a great agent, and I love him, but the man needs an off switch."

"I couldn't agree more," she replied. Leaning over, she pressed her lips to his. "Thank you for that."

A few minutes later, they were pulling into the line of cars that led up to the red carpet. When it was their turn to get out, Reed went first and then turned to help her.

The reporters were already shouting, camera flashes going off. They paused and posed together a few times, and then separately. Finally, it was time for the quick interview portion right up against the velvet rope.

"Tell us, Teagan, are you pregnant?" The reporter from TMZ placed a microphone in her face, his cameraman leaning in behind him. "The world wants confirmation!"

Reed wanted to tell them to back the hell up, but Teagan held her ground well.

She glanced up at him, a shy smile on her face. "We're not answering questions yet."

"So, there *are* questions to answer?" the reporter pressed further.

Reed placed his arm behind Teagan's back, steering her down the row. "The lady said all she wanted to say."

While he definitely wanted to shout their news from the rooftops, he was going to let her take the lead on when she wanted to reveal her pregnancy. After all, she was still pretty early along, so he could understand her caution.

"Reed Scott! Teagan Reynolds!" A reporter from E! Flagged them down next. "We've been dying to know—are you two a couple?"

Teagan's face lit up, clearly unable to hide her happiness. She looked up at Reed. "I'll let you answer this one."

Fuck, yes. "I've never been more in love in my life," Reed replied to the reporter, wrapping his arm back around her waist. "So, yes."

The reporter swooned, placing her hand on her chest. "That is so romantic. And all this happened on the set of *Break Down?*"

"I've been in love with Teagan for more than a decade but

Break Down brought us back together." He figured he'd throw Jason a bone.

Teagan leaned her head against his shoulder, curling into his side affectionately. Damn, he loved every second of having her pressed against him.

"Will we be hearing wedding bells anytime soon?" The reporter held out the microphone to them again, her hunger clear.

Reed laughed and shook his head. "I actually proposed to her earlier tonight, but she said no."

"What?" The reporter looked both confused and crushed, then turned to Teagan. "Why did you turn it down?"

Teagan shrugged. "He deserved it."

"She's right about that," Reed confirmed, still laughing. "Don't worry. I'll keep proposing until she says yes."

The reporter swooned again. "You guys are too cute. I can't even handle it."

She let them go and Teagan leaned in to whisper to him. "Jason's going to kill you for saying that."

"Probably," Reed laughed. "But it's true. I'm not going anywhere, Teagan."

She surveyed his face, like she was looking for it all to be a lie. He wasn't sure what he could do to convince her that this was real, and he was here to stay, but he was sure as hell going to keep trying every day until she trusted him again.

"I think I know that," she replied slowly, but the hesitation was unmistakable.

Reed took her hand, squeezing it and leading her further down the red carpet.

CHAPTER THIRTY-ONE

"ARE you going to be okay here alone?" Reed whispered to her, his hand on her knee.

Teagan nodded. "Go. You're the star."

He smiled, placed a kiss on her cheek, then stood and moved toward the aisle. He was heading backstage to prepare for the question and answer panel with journalists about the movie. Teagan watched him go, trying not to be too obvious about admiring his backside. He looked freaking amazing in his tuxedo.

When he got to the aisle, he turned back to face her and winked.

She could feel her cheeks heating as she blushed, smiling back at him. Even in little actions like that—him taking a moment to give her that attention—was a new trait for him. The way he publicly professed his love for her at any chance he got...she didn't know what to do with that. He'd never before been the type to put his own image aside to prioritize her.

The man she'd dated in college had been loving and sweet, but he'd still been an early twenties male who tended to err on the side of selfish more often than not. At the time, she had never really noticed because she'd been the same age and the same level (or lack thereof) of maturity. But the last eight years had been a growing process for her, both forced through circumstances, and naturally through age.

When they'd first met again at the beginning of filming *Break Down*, she had been able to tell that he'd grown some. He was definitely trying to change, wanting to change...but had he? She'd not seen enough proof back then to dive headfirst. Her instinct had been telling her to hold back, and it turned out her instinct was spot on. The moment they'd hit a roadblock—one stupid tabloid article—he'd gone right back to his old ways.

So, as much as she wanted to believe him this time, she was terrified for the moment when things got too tough, too raw, too real, too hard...and then he'd leave. He'd disappoint her again.

She wasn't sure she could survive it, and she had someone else to think about now.

Teagan sighed. A pressure in her abdomen had her deciding to take a bathroom break before the festivities started. She maneuvered down the row of chairs and headed out of the theatre. The ushers sent someone to fill her seat while she was gone—such an odd practice she still wasn't used to.

"Hey!" Steele, her makeup artist spotted her in the lobby. "How's the movie?"

"It just finished and they're starting commentary and panels," she explained, still heading in the direction of the bathroom. "I'm taking a bathroom break."

"Oh, perfect," Steele replied. "Gives me a chance to touch up your makeup."

"Be my guest." Teagan motioned for her to follow, but she definitely needed to go to the bathroom quickly. She was already feeling a pain in her abdomen, pressure on her bladder, and was starting to panic that she wouldn't make it. She'd barely had anything to drink, so she wasn't sure why she had to go so badly.

Rushing into the stall, she reached for the bottom hem of her long dress and began to pull it up her legs. A red smear across the inner side of her ankle caught her attention, and as she continued lifting her dress, she realized it went all the way up her leg.

Teagan's vision began to blur as a lightheaded sensation assaulted her. Reaching between her legs, she confirmed her fears and her legs began to shake. She was bleeding.

"Steele?" she called out.

"I'm all set up when you're ready," Steele called back. "I've got a gorgeous new set of brushes you're going to love."

"Steele..." Teagan's voice trembled, and she clutched the railing in the bathroom stall in an attempt to stay standing. "I need help."

"Oh, you need someone to hold your dress?" Steele's shoes came up at the bottom of the stall. "Unlock the door. I got you, girl. Wouldn't be my first time."

Teagan reached out and clicked the lock, but her legs gave out and she slid to the hard tile floor the moment the door swung open. Everything was beginning to feel fuzzy, and cramps were beginning to set in, making her gasp in pain.

"Oh my, God! Teagan!" Steele shrieked, quickly scurrying to her side and holding Teagan against her chest. "What the hell happened? Holy shit...are you pregnant?"

Teagan nodded slowly, but she wasn't sure she could find her words. "Call...call Reed."

She closed her eyes, concentrating on breathing through the pain, or at least trying to...until everything went black.

CHAPTER THIRTY-TWO

"TEAG?"

Her eyes slowly blinked open, taking in the scene around her. She was in a stark white hospital room, packed full of her entire family.

Simone was inches from her face, staring at her with concern. "You awake?" she asked.

Teagan nodded her head, but didn't reply. The events of the last few minutes—*was it minutes? Hours?*—began coming back to her. Her hand flew to her stomach. "The baby?! Is the baby okay?"

Teagan's mother grabbed her hand, squeezing it. "The baby is fine," she assured her. "It was some irregular bleeding, but you're going to be okay."

Relief flooded her at the news. The thought of losing her baby had hit her harder than she'd even expected. She'd only known about this baby's existence for a few weeks, but already there was no doubt that she wanted the little peanut more than anything in the world. She rubbed her hand across her stomach. *It's okay, baby. I'll take care of you. Nothing is going to happen to you.*

"You'll need to be on bed rest for the remainder of the pregnancy," Aria told her from where she was standing at the end of the hospital bed. "But they think everything will be fine."

Teagan looked around the room, searching for the one face she really wanted to see. Reed wasn't there. She wasn't sure why she was surprised. It wasn't the first time she'd looked around a hospital room and hoped to see him there.

She swallowed, trying to keep her grief at bay. She couldn't let it consume her when she had to stay positive for her baby. It was just that...things had felt different this time. He'd felt different, and she'd slowly been deciding to trust him, and trust that this time he was going to stay.

He was going to be there. God, she'd really thought he'd be here.

"These doctors are fucking stupid," a deep voice growled, suddenly entering the hospital room. "We're bringing in a specialist."

"Reed?" Teagan gasped at the sight.

"Babe, you're awake!" Reed rushed to the side of her bed, and her mother quickly moved out of the way, patting him on the shoulder.

"We'll give you two some time together," her mother said. "Come on, guys. Let's go down to the cafeteria for a bite."

Teagan noted the sweet gesture, surprised her family was seeming to embrace Reed.

He squeezed her hand, placing a kiss on her cheek. "How are you feeling?"

Tears welled in her eyes and she couldn't stop them from sliding down her cheeks. Sobs wrenched from her throat, and she couldn't stop herself from crying. Not just small tears, but complete bawling and shoulder shaking as she tried to catch her breath.

Ironically, she wasn't sad. She wasn't even hurt. She was relieved.

"Teag, what's wrong?" Reed ran his hand down the side of her face, cupping her cheek. "Don't cry. The baby is okay. You're going to be okay. I'm bringing in a specialist just to make sure, but you and Peanut are both going to be fine."

She shook her head, trying to swallow the lump in her throat. "It's not that. I know that. I mean, I'm so relieved. If anything had happened to this baby..." Her hand rubbed her stomach again. "I couldn't survive it."

He nodded his head in agreement. "I couldn't either." His brows furrowed and he squeezed her hand. "Why are you crying then?"

She wiped the tears from her cheeks. "I woke up, and I didn't see you. I...I thought you didn't come." The memories of years ago after her accident flooded her, and how devastated she'd been every day that she didn't hear from him. "I thought you'd left."

Reed stood and carefully climbed onto the bed next to her, taking care not to mess with the wires and tubes connected to her. He cuddled her to his chest, and she gratefully pressed against him, craving the contact.

"I know I haven't done anything to deserve your trust, Teag. I know I've earned your fear that I would leave," he began, kissing the top of her head and rubbing his hand across her back. "But I meant it when I said I'm all in this time. I meant it when I said that I'll spend every day of the rest of my life proving that to you."

Teagan sniffed, the tears beginning to flow again.

"I love you, Teag. I love our baby. I'm going to love our life together—even if we live in the suburbs behind a white picket fence and I spend my days driving kids around to different sports and activities. I don't care what we do, or where we are. I just want to be with you."

She wrapped her arms around him, hugging him tightly. "Yes."

Leaning back slightly, he looked in her eyes. "Yes?"

"Yes, I'll marry you."

Reed smiled, his green eyes sparkling. "That's the best news I've ever heard."

"But, I have one condition," she continued. "I want to get married right now."

His brows furrowed. "Uh, babe, we're in the hospital."

"They have a chapel and chaplains here." She grinned, squeezing him tighter. "I've already done the wedding planning thing, and I'm never doing it again. I'm also not going to put myself through the torture of being terrified you're not going to show up again."

"Babe, I would *never* do that to you again," he assured her, kissing her temple and squeezing her tighter. "Never. I know I don't have a leg to stand on, but I can promise you with everything in me that *that* is not who I am anymore."

"I know," she replied, leaning in and kissing him gently, brushing her lips over his. "I believe you. I see that that isn't who you are. But...it's still a thought that's going to cross my mind. Not just about you showing up, but the memory of the accident afterwards. It's too much pain, and I don't want something as wonderful as our wedding day to be tainted by the memories of the past."

"That makes sense. Okay, let's do it." Reed reached into his pocket and pulled out a small ring box. "It's a good thing I've been carrying this around for a while."

Teagan's eyes widened. "Reed..."

He opened the box and the most beautiful diamond ring she'd ever seen stared back at her. "I can't wait to marry you, Teag. I don't care if it's in a big church or in a hospital bed. I just want to be with you. I want to raise this baby together. I want to start the life we should have had years ago."

He took the ring from the box, and she held out her hand. Slowly, he slid it on her finger. She couldn't take her eyes off it, but then he kissed her and she wound her arms around his neck. His tongue slid across her lower lip and she parted for him.

"I love you, Reed," she finally admitted, whispering between kisses. "I love you so much."

"I love you, Teag." He kissed her harder. "Now, let's go get married."

Teagan smiled, and despite the fact that she was in the hospital, this was the best wedding day she could ever have imagined.

EPILOGUE

18 MONTHS LATER

"Cut!" Mario waved his hands in the air. "That was fucking perfect!"

Reed glanced over at his wife, grinning. "You were amazing."

"I had a great partner," Teagan replied, blowing him a kiss and then heading off the set. "I need to pump."

"The miracle of motherhood and all that," Mario commented, watching her go. He turned to Reed, who was now stretching after just having finished an insanely complicated dance scene in *Break Down 2*. He and Teagan were both in starring roles, and she was absolutely amazing in hers. "How's fatherhood treating you?"

He couldn't even put into words how wonderful being married to the love of his life and raising their child together was. Reed hadn't known such bliss was even possible. Every morning, he woke up and looked over at his sleeping wife cuddling an old snoring cat, and then in the crib next to the bed with their ten-month old daughter, and it was by far the most beautiful scene he could imagine.

Teagan was the best mom he'd ever seen, and she spent every

free moment loving on Piper Simone Scott. She barely ever let her out of her sight unless they were working, even insisting the crib stay in their room despite the fact that they had a huge, professionally decorated nursery right down the hall.

Reed didn't mind, because he loved having his daughter around too. But even more than that, he loved seeing his wife happy. He loved seeing her hold their daughter, and the way her face lit up with love when she looked at her.

"Piper is perfect," he admitted to the director. "She's definitely got me wrapped around her fingers already."

"Baby girls will do that." Mario chuckled. "My daughters are the love of my life."

That was exactly how he felt.

"How's my favorite star?" Jason Allen walked up to the two men. "You guys killed that scene. This movie's going to be a bigger hit than the first."

Reed hoped, but it was hard to top the fandom that had surrounded the first movie. The press credited his relationship with Teagan for a lot of its success, because the PR around them had been an amazing marketing tool. He didn't care one bit about that though. All he wanted was to come to work every day and do his best, then go home every night with his wife and be the best father and husband he could be.

"Thanks, Jason," he replied, shaking his hand. "What do you have for me today?"

"Actually, nothing for you. I've got a new contract for your wife on deck, though."

Reed laughed, feeling an overwhelming sense of pride in Teagan's success over the last year and a half. "Is she your biggest client now?"

Jason nodded his head, grinning. "She seriously is. You've been upstaged, kid."

"Good," Reed said. "She deserves it. She's insanely talented."

"One of the best I've ever seen," Jason admitted. "Where did she go? I've got to talk to her about this contract."

"She's pumping."

Jason grimaced. "Uh, I'll...come back later. How's Piper doing anyway?"

"She's beautiful." Reed pulled out his phone and began showing off photos of the tiny baby.

"What an angel," Jason agreed. "Well, I'll come back later today to talk with her. Get back to shooting."

"Yes, sir." Reed saluted with his middle finger against his forehead and a wide grin. "I'll make you proud."

Rolling his eyes, Jason shook his hand again then headed off the set.

Reed glanced toward the hallway to the dressing rooms, and decided to go find his wife. He strolled along the corridor until he saw the room with her name on it, then walked in without knocking. Teagan was standing in front of the vanity mirror, running her hands down her sides. Concern etched her face.

"Hey, babe." Reed closed the door behind him. "What's wrong?"

She blushed, her cheeks flushing red. "Oh. I was just fussing over this baby weight. I can't seem to get rid of it."

Reed scoffed, coming up behind her and wrapping his arms around her. "You've clearly lost your mind because every single part of your body is the sexiest thing I've ever seen."

She turned to face him, wrapping her arms around his neck. "Is that so?"

"Mmmhm." He kissed down her neck and nipped her flesh. "In fact, you're so sexy that I think we should lock the door."

Teagan giggled and squeezed out of his arms. She quickly stepped to the door, turned the lock, and then returned to his side, already wiggling out of her leggings. Reed growled and began unbuckling his pants. Once undressed, he gripped her ass and laid her on the dressing room couch.

"Remember the last time we did it like this?" he teased, sliding his fingers across her slit. She was already soaked for him, and he could barely stand the wait.

Teagan moaned and bucked her hips against his hand. "Mmm...that's how we got Piper."

Reed pulled down her shirt and kissed the swell of her breast, taking mind to keep away from her too sensitive nipples. "Maybe we should try again," he whispered, kissing up her chest and capturing her lips with his. "Maybe Piper needs a little sister or brother."

She laughed and grabbed his hips, pulling him toward her center. She gripped his cock and guided him to her. "I guess we'll see what happens."

He growled, loving that answer. There was nothing more he wanted than to have a million babies with this woman. Plunging inside her, he groaned at the sensation of her body pulsing around his. They moved together in rhythm, her arms anchored around his neck and his hands underneath her ass.

Reed slid his tongue across her lower lip, pushing her toward her climax as his tongue dove into her mouth.

"Oh, God...Reed." Teagan moaned against his lips. "I'm so close."

He reached between their bodies, rubbing his thumb against her clit until her body began to shake and tremble against him. "Come for me, Teag..."

"Mmm," she moaned against his shoulder, muffling her voice as she clung to him.

He felt his own climax approaching as he thrust harder, then he pulled her against him to be as deep as possible as they both unraveled around one another. Gasping, they stayed wrapped together, only separating enough to kiss.

Reed brushed his lips over hers, placing small kisses against her as he reveled in how beautiful she was, and how desperately he loved her. "God, Teag...you're amazing."

She ran her fingers down the side of his face, then kissed him again. "I have a great partner," she repeated. "And I love him so much."

"I've loved you forever..." He peppered her face with kisses, and she laughed, batting him away. "And I'll love you for always."

He quoted their favorite children's book that they'd been reading to Piper, even though it always made him cry by the end. "Thanks for never giving up on me, Teag."

Teagan smiled. "Thanks for never letting me."

WHAT TO READ NEXT

The next standalone novel in this Hollywood romance series, **Sheer: A Hollywood Romance**, releases on September 4, 2018.

Preorder at your local or online book retailer today!

ALSO BY SARAH ROBINSON

The Photographer Trilogy

(*Romantic Suspense*)

Tainted Bodies

Tainted Pictures

Untainted

The Photographer Trilogy Boxset (includes deleted scene!)

Forbidden Rockers Series

(*Rockstar Romances*)

Logan's Story: A Prequel Novella

Her Forbidden Rockstar

Rocker Christmas: A Logan & Caroline Holiday Novella

Logan Clay: The Box Set

Kavanagh Legends Series

(*MMA Fighter Standalone Romances*)

Breaking a Legend

Saving a Legend

Becoming a Legend

Chasing a Legend

Kavanagh Christmas

Nudes Series

ABOUT THE AUTHOR

Sarah Robinson is the Top 10 Barnes & Noble and Amazon Bestselling Author of multiple series and standalone novels, including *The Photographer Trilogy, Kavanagh Legends* series, the *Forbidden Rockers* series, and *Not a Hero: A Marine Romance*. A native of Washington, D.C., Robinson has both her bachelor's and master's degrees in forensic and clinical psychology, and works in a crisis stabilization center.

Follow the Author on Social Media

booksbysarahrobinson.net

subscribepage.com/sarahrobinsonnewsletter
facebook.com/booksbysarahrobinson
twitter.com/booksby_sarah
goodreads.com/booksbysarahrobinson
instagram.com/booksbysarahrobinson
Snapchat: @booksbysarahrob